THE I

MYSTERIES

www.liffeyrivers.com

OTHER BOOKS BY BRENNA BRIGGS

The Mystery of the Sparkling Solo Dress Crown

The Mystery of the Winking Judge

The Secret of the Mountain of the Moon

In the Shadow of the Serpent

The Alaskan Sun

The Mystery of the Pointing Dog

Four Mini Mysteries

Non-Liffey Rivers Series:

Mothers Addicted To Irish Dancing: MAIDS

For Fiona —

Liffey Rivers

The Mystery of the Whispering Trees

by

Brenna Briggs

from

Brenna Briggs
2019

Brockagh Books
Mineral Point, Wisconsin 53565

ISBN-10: 1548797979
ISBN-13: 9781548797973

A MURMUR IN THE TREES

A Murmur in the Trees-to note-
Not loud enough-for Wind-
A Star-not far enough to seek-
Nor near enough-to find

EMILY DICKINSON
1830-1886
American Poet

MORNING MADNESS

The vampire rumor was spreading faster than an out of control forest fire. Erupting without warning on a predawn gray November morning, it had created mass confusion and in many cases, panic, in Mineral Point, Wisconsin.

Superintendent of Schools, Eva Blatz, had retreated to her office, where she sat staring out a large picture window, counting the buzzards circling the Mineral Point water tower.

There were seven.

Blatz's frazzled secretary, Marilyn McDonald, was diverting all of the calls she did not recognize to the live answering service the school system paid dearly for, but rarely used.

Ms. Blatz now faced the most significant challenge of her career: how to classify and then manage the aftermath of the event that had taken place earlier that morning.

1

Eva Blatz was painfully aware that all 'emergencies' were expected to be dealt with expeditiously. Code for 'fix it immediately,' or else…

The Superintendent was almost positive that what had taken place that morning in Mineral Point should not be labeled a 'natural emergency.' There had not been a tornado or snow storm or flash flood in Iowa County.

However, it also seemed possible, that whatever had happened that morning, might not have been a 'manmade' emergency either.

Because, if it actually *had* been a confrontation with a vampire, it would be a supernatural emergency.

What is wrong with me? Vampires are in books of fiction and horror films, she reminded herself.

The buzzard count went up two. There were now nine buzzards on the water tower circuit. Eva's mind wandered back to childhood Halloweens in Mineral Point—damp leaves raked into curbside piles, smoke ghosts swirling around her ankles and the scary tingle in the air that started at sundown.

She had never thought about this before, but there had usually been a disproportionately large number of trick-or-treating Count Draculas in their plastic, store-bought costumes, going door to door for candy. The fake blood running down from the corners of their little mouths had always given her the creeps.

All her graduate degrees and the extensive licensing requirements she had happily undertaken to become a 'Superintendent of Schools,' had never once addressed how to handle a 'paranormal event.'

Whatever it was that had occurred, her district was now in the 'responsive' mode and she must make sure it led to a full recovery.

Immediately.

Eva knew that there were many underemployed educators in Wisconsin who would love to have her job.

She could almost see them now, soaring overhead like majestic hawks on strong currents of wind, biding their time, waiting to swoop down into her office, where she was cowering like a little field mouse.

Perhaps the School District's Safety, Emergency and Post-Incident teams might have some idea of what to do?

The Chief of Police had rushed to the scene of the event and would certainly be contacting her soon to explain exactly what it was that the students thought they had experienced outside The Foundry Books that morning. Hopefully, that would put an end to this nonsense. *After all, it was only a senior class prank,* she told herself.

All of the Mineral Point schools had manned their hallways with volunteers from clubs and community organizations. The doors at the schools were being protected by specially trained police officers from Madison.

Primary school teachers were instructed to conduct morning recess periods indoors, even though this early November day had been unseasonably warm.

3

Parents and caregivers raced to the schools to pick up their children. Shops shut down and High Street was mostly deserted by noon.

The six very traumatized senior high school students waiting for their school bus that morning, could not all agree on the details as to exactly what had taken place. They had been interviewed separately, so they would not influence one another's stories.

The basic core of all their narratives, however, was that early that morning, someone, or as freshman Robert Thomas had blurted out, **"something,"** had deposited an unidentified object in the tiny wooden haiku box on The Foundry Books' front porch.

The pagoda-like receptacle resembled a birdhouse, and was a repository for local poets to leave their latest haiku poems to be shared with others.

The three high school sophomores, who had been standing at the corner of Commerce and Fountain Streets, described seeing a skinny, emaciated-looking old man on the bookstore side of the street. They said that they could see his stick-like figure clearly when he had passed by them under a street light.

Jennifer Tassone had reported seeing a withered old man, suspended several inches above the sidewalk, moving slowly towards The Foundry Books.

Sally Nolder disagreed and said that she had seen an emaciated old man limping along with both of his feet planted firmly on the sidewalk.

Yvonne Gonzalez had confirmed the creepy old man. However, she said he had looked like a skeleton

4

surfer riding a wave, arms outstretched for balance as he coasted towards The Foundry Books, several feet above the ground.

Freshman Billy Barnes, who had moved to Mineral Point only a few weeks ago, said that he had been approaching the bus stop from the opposite direction on Commerce Street. He recounted seeing a young man with long dark hair, racing past a hideous skeletal creature.

He said that the young man had stopped suddenly, looked around furtively in every direction and then sprinted up the Foundry's porch steps. Barnes said he saw the man put something inside the haiku house but he could not see well enough to make out what it was.

A sixth student, Junior Class President Julia Brick, known to be a very sensible young lady on track to be her class valedictorian, also remembered seeing a tall young man with coal black hair trailing behind him like a banner waving in the wind, running past a jaundiced old man limping along with a cane on the sidewalk. She reported that both men were definitely moving along the sidewalk with their feet firmly on the ground.

Julia Brick also reported that the running man jumped up onto the porch like he was in a Super Mario Brothers game and immediately put something inside the haiku house. She had not been able to see what it was.

All of the students had agreed that a plume of black smoke materialized on the bookstore's porch under its night light and then quickly transformed into a giant man wearing a long black cape.

This grand finale was followed by a powerful blast of frigid wind which roared down Commerce Street, causing the students' teeth to chatter as they ran up Fountain Street, away from the nightmarish specter.

Observing the panicked state that these seemingly normal high school students were in, and taking into account the twenty 911 calls he had received, the Mineral Point Chief of Police hurried to the haiku drop house, hoping that, annoying as it seemed, the whole thing was some sort of practical joke.

Or perhaps just a group of bored students playing 'Pokémon Go' who were now experiencing some kind of mass hallucination, like in a virtual reality game.

When the Chief arrived at The Foundry Books, he was distressed to see that a large group of townspeople had already gathered.

How that had happened so quickly, he attributed to the coming of mobile phones. Ever since the advent of cell phones, land lines had almost become obsolete. Information was now available almost instantly to the people who lived in Mineral Point.

Thus, even before a police investigation could be formally launched, almost everyone in town thought they already knew exactly what had happened and rumors ran rampant from the get-go.

This greatly impeded any kind of fresh, impartial approach to solving a crime. The Chief had long ago made a point not to engage in speculation with the locals before he did his own investigation.

He was grateful that here in Mineral Point, there was very little crime. Senior class pranks were about as complicated as his police work had been to date—except for last November, when the Rivers family had attracted Federal agents and more chaos than he could have ever imagined. He had been very relieved when that stressful event was over.

The Chief roped off The Foundry Books' porch with yellow 'Caution Keep Out' tape, put on latex gloves, aimed his camera and began his investigation. Trying to ignore the onlookers, who apparently were going to remain there indefinitely, watching him work, he muttered an expletive to himself.

Inside the haiku box, he found what appeared to be a haiku poem in 5-7-5 syllable format. It was written on what looked like old calves parchment—velum.

Only here, the Chief smiled, taking tweezers from his satchel to hold the old paper as he read words written in dark red ink, or red berries goo, or possibly blood, *would someone like me know that this is a haiku poem because it is written in three lines with 5 syllables on the first line, 7 syllables on the second line, and 5 syllables again on the third line:* Trees are whispering

darkness will swallow the sun

When Wendigo comes

He deposited the haiku inside the plastic folder in his evidence satchel and looked again into the dark little box house.

Next, he removed a carefully folded 8 by 10 inch sheet of copy paper that had what appeared to be two Japanese characters generated by a computer:

復讐

There was also an overpowering stench coming from the haiku box that made him gag and a medium size box turtle.

He carefully placed the turtle in the outer catch net attached to the satchel, closed the tiny haiku house door and removed his gloves.

HAIKU HOUSE

CONTEMPLATION

Liffey Rivers gathered her long, light brown hair into a ponytail and pulled it through a grody hair tie that her dog Max had obviously used as a chew toy when he could not find a sock.

She unrolled her brand-new, magenta-colored yoga mat on the squishy patches of yellowing grass between two old ginkgo trees in her backyard.

On the day that Liffey had told her Aunt Jean that she had been meditating regularly, the first thing her aunt had said was: "What color is your yoga mat?"

When Liffey answered: "dark blue," her aunt had shuddered and advised her naïve niece to "empower herself with color."

Three days later, her aunt presented Liffey with a purplish-red yoga mat, explaining that: "this particular shade of magenta, represents universal harmony and emotional balance."

After doing her stretches and ten deep knee bends, Liffey assumed the lotus position, facing the forest bordering her family's property. She began breathing deeply and centering herself.

After meditating for some time, the ground beneath her started vibrating—again. These earth tremors did not bother her very much anymore because they had been happening on and off now for the past three weeks and so far, no one had reported any earthquakes or fallen into a sink hole.

Ann Strong, her Earth Science teacher, would have been all over the earthquake topic by now if there had actually been one here in southwestern Wisconsin.

As far as Liffey knew, there was no fracking going on either. She was aware that there were abandoned lead mines underneath Mineral Point, but according to her father, Robert Rivers, there were no working ones. They had closed down permanently in the 1930's.

No one, including her parents, little brother Neil, or classmates at the Mineral Point Senior High School, had ever talked about any ground vibrations.

At first, Liffey thought that she might be getting sick and was having pre-fever shakes. However, since she had not become ill, this had to be ruled out.

Eventually, she resigned herself to the fact that, like many of the uninvited people and events that kept barging in and out of her life, there apparently *was* no explanation. Then the tremors had suddenly stopped.

Until now.

Faraway, in the densely wooded area bordering her yard, Liffey could hear a coyote screaming and making other-worldly noises.

She panicked for a moment until she remembered that her little terrier, Max, was inside the house, asleep on the living room couch. She breathed easily again and resumed her quest for enlightenment. A heady scent of decaying yellow mums drifted towards her, making her drowsy.

Her eyes opened wide when ginkgo leaves brushed by her face, like fluttering butterflies. She enjoyed watching them landing and blending in with the yellow petals on her mother's big leaf ligularia plants.

Liffey's mother, Maeve, had told her, when she asked what kind of trees had "such delicate fan-shaped leaves," that temples throughout Asia, "often have gingko trees just like ours planted around them to ward off evil."

"Many ginkgoes in the world today are thousands of years old, Liffey. We know from fossil impressions that ginkgoes lived during the dinosaur age. There is a ginkgo tree in China right now that is known to be at least three thousand, five hundred years old. Ginkgo trees are living fossils—like our own redwoods and sequoia trees out west in the United States."

Since that conversation with her mother, Liffey had felt very safe here, meditating on the ground under her own ginkgo trees, hoping they were protecting her from malevolent spirits and evil human beings.

She breathed slowly, trying to get back into her meditation groove. Instead, she began to twitch as she tried in vain to shake off the creepy crawly sensations which were now moving up and down her spine.

11

I am just imagining this, she told herself again, for the umpteenth time. *It has got to be a seriously bad case of nerves. I am sitting in my own backyard. Places don't get much safer than your own backyard.*

She never told anyone, but for the last few weeks, she was certain that she had heard voices coming up from the ground while she was meditating.

The voices had recently stopped but she had been unable to get rid of a deep foreboding that something was wrong.

Dangerously wrong.

"There are six ginkgo trees in Hiroshima, Japan, Liffey," Maeve's gentle voice continued inside Liffey's head, "that somehow survived the atom bomb the United States dropped on it during World War II."

Loud snoring jolted Liffey awake, snapping her out of her dream-like state. She could feel her eyes being drawn upward, to a nun in a white habit, hovering above the two ginkgo trees like wispy smoke rising from a chimney.

In the split second it had taken Liffey to blink her eyes, trying to focus, the nun had shape-shifted into an enormous, transparent face in the woods.

Her expressionless eyes looked out from behind leafless, intertwining tree branches, reminding Liffey of the network of veins, arteries and capillaries in her body's circulatory system.

She blinked again and the face was gone.

She had obviously been dreaming.

TWO BOX TURTLES

Liffey filed the absurd vampire rumor circulating at school that morning in the, 'This So Never Happened' lobe of her brain. Then, she considered whether or not her Aunt Jean might be right about having a magenta-colored yoga mat.

Maybe color really could empower people?

How clueless did the senior class think the rest of the school was? she thought, grasping a floating ginkgo leaf before it drifted out of reach.

At the moment, Liffey had other things to worry about. Such as, whether or not her father, who had recently become the definition of an ouch nerve, was considering relocating again.

Since Robert Rivers' stress level was at least 100%, she realized that it was entirely possible that this was precisely what was happening.

After all, his carefully designed underground safe house had been a complete fiasco last November after she had tried to set the timer on its automatic security system. Instead, she had accidentally locked everyone, except her father, inside the compound for twenty-four hours.

There had also been a shocking, unexpected enemy with a loaded gun, locked inside the underground safe house with them.

This had created a very nerve-wracking, as well as dangerous, situation.

Liffey was not sure she would ever be able to trust anyone other than her family and John ever again.

Fortunately, her friend John had been able to fix the locked door problem using a bobby pin he found in her mother's purse, while a very impatient group of Wisconsin National Guardsmen, Federal agents and two circling helicopters from Interpol, waited for lock specialists to arrive so they could enter the Rivers' subterranean compound and rescue everyone—and hopefully capture an elusive counterfeiter.

What had really happened down in the safe house, was something Liffey consciously did not allow herself to think about.

It was still too painful. If it had not all been so ridiculous, it might have been considered a disaster.

It was apparent to Liffey that her worn-out father considered it to have been the latter.

Or was it the former? Liffey could *never* remember how those two exasperating words should be used.

She made up her wandering, meditative mind, that she would never use either of those confusing words again.

She really needed to exert some control over her life anyway. She would start doing that right now by never using the words 'former' and 'latter' together again.

Ever.

It was just too much to think about.

Liffey drew in long breaths of balmy, end of Indian Summer air. She exhaled slowly, using the advanced 'Om' meditation she had learned in her Aunt Jean's School of Life.

She hoped that the acute embarrassment she had unintentionally caused her much-loved, well-meaning father by first, letting her friend John solve Robert Rivers' safe house's lockdown emergency, and then, sneaking off to investigate with Susan and John and Aunt Jean in her pink Cadillac, was not irreparable.

Liffey felt badly about it now. At the time, her father, in his own way, had quietly admitted that her actions had probably saved his life and possibly even prevented the collapse of the entire British monetary system.

You would think that might have counted for something! she thought, in what had now become a non-meditating, extremely irritable frame of mind.

As usual, Liffey was forbidden to talk about what had really happened with anyone outside of the family, except Susan Scott and John Bergman, who had both been there with her throughout the whole safe house ordeal.

They too had been ordered to remain silent by the FBI, the CIA and some other Federal agency Liffey could never remember the name of.

Liffey understood all the secrecy stuff, but now she was not even allowed to go back down into her own safe house to relax with friends because it was still, after all these months—a year now—considered to be an international 'crime scene' and had to be preserved.

Interpol had never divulged for what purpose it *had* to be "preserved" and Liffey was sick of it.

What good was living above the most amazing underground complex in southwestern Wisconsin if you couldn't even walk through one of its many secret entrances?

Or use the underground tunnel from the shed?

Or the secret panel in their dining room?

Robert Rivers turned beet red when she had asked him if she could at least use their family's secret place, since it was "not-so-secret anymore," for a surprise party for the Bergman brothers and Sinéad McGowan when they arrived from O'Hare Airport.

Liffey's escalating and, if she were to be honest with herself, somewhat petty and definitely self-pitying thoughts, were interrupted by the startling appearance of two large box turtles.

They were inching their way out from underneath the bigleaf ligularia plants and squeezing through the gaps between some of the field stones.

These four-foot-high plants, with their clusters of yellow daisy-like flowers, had been planted to match the now yellowing ginkgo trees' leaves and yellow mums. Liffey had not known until this yard, that her mother liked the color yellow so much.

Seeing just one box turtle would have been very unusual because Liffey had been taught in biology class that box turtles were an endangered species in Wisconsin. So she had never expected to actually ever see one—let alone two box turtles, up close like this. *How could this be happening?*

She knew they were box turtles because of their distinctive shells—*were they black shells with yellow lines or yellow shells with black lines?*

Liffey yawned, smiled contentedly and stood up, meditating about how meditating sometimes gave her profound insights.

Either way you looked at their shells—all black with yellow patterns, or all yellow with black patterns, it was very exciting to see two real box turtles in her backyard.

This unprecedented appearance of the box turtles in the Rivers' backyard became even more intriguing when the two turtles abruptly stopped their forward march. Simultaneously, they stretched their leathery necks, seemingly looking at the ginkgo trees.

If Liffey did not know better, she might think that these turtles were actually communicating with these ginkgo trees.

She returned to the lotus position on her yoga mat.

What was going on? Maybe the turtles saw the nun?

Unexpectedly, Liffey had goose bumps when she could tell that the ginkgoes' leaves were moving ever so slightly—almost imperceptibly.

However, there *was* no wind interacting with the mums or bigleaf ligularia plants. Nothing was moving in the yard except for the ginkgoes' leaves.

Liffey's hands began to tingle. It felt like there was a slight electrical current moving through them.

Could these backyard ginkgo trees be *communicating* with the turtles? She was obviously imagining things.

She had watched a video in Middle School a few years ago, about how trees were thought to be able to communicate in some way with other trees, by using a complicated network of underground fungi growing out from their roots.

But they certainly did not speak 'Turtle!'

And vice-versa.

And what had happened to the floating nun?

Liffey did not dwell on the floating nun illusion. It was too much to think about all at once. She had heard that, while meditating, it was often good to combine 'reflection' with 'speculation' but it never seemed to work for her.

She always seemed to end up getting preoccupied, reflecting about how words like 'neither and nor' and 'former and latter' worked together.

And why anyone should care?

She had also been trying not to keep 'speculating' about 'why' and 'how' so many impossible things, which should not *really* ever happen to anyone, *had* happened to her.

She would have to say, if anyone ever actually asked her, "Why do these seemingly impossible things keep happening?" that she did not care to 'speculate' about it.

Or should that be 'reflect' upon it?

Or 'reflect' about it?

Or *neither* speculate *nor* reflect?

Liffey often had the urge to stand perfectly still and scream in place for exactly one minute.

Like the noon siren did every day.

Maybe she could actually get paid for screaming every day at noon in Mineral Point? She could invest in a sound system and record it.

However, if she did scream for one full minute every day of the week, she was likely to lose her voice entirely. Perhaps permanently.

But still, it might be good to vent every day at noon.

Ever since St. Louis, she felt like she had been walking on a tightrope.

It was not easy tip-toeing through her life this way.

Every single day.

Waking up in the morning, wondering if this would be the day that 'he' would find her again and she would finally fall into the abyss that was on standby, waiting for Liffey Rivers to drop in.

So, if her father *was* thinking about pulling out of Mineral Point and moving to the North Pole next time for a better hiding place, she supposed it would work out.

As long as John Bergman was allowed to visit. It would be a hard-sell to his mother though.

His mother thought she was "dangerous" and her son would not be safe around her, even in a place like southwestern Wisconsin.

Liffey wished she could laugh about this. But deep inside, she knew his mother might be right.

She took some pictures of the visiting turtles with her phone and texted her own mother about how crazy this whole turtle thing was.

When she had finished stretching, she went back into her house to collect her backpack before setting out to meet her friend Susan Scott at the Red Rooster Café.

THE BIRDMAN
OF MINERAL POINT

Working with his high-powered Magni-Pros extra-wide magnifying glass, Chief Smith scrutinized the sinister haiku poem and the oriental symbols.

The fact that it had become a rite-of-passage for seniors at the local high school to orchestrate farewell pranks, wearied him.

The more outrageous the stunt, the more prestige was bestowed upon the perpetrators—and always, it seemed, at his own expense.

The Chief made a temporary environment for the box turtle inside a large plastic laundry basket. Feeling like a little child excited by his lucky turtle discovery, he poured water into a shallow aluminum tray 'lake' and placed twigs and leaves among the pebbles and rocks which he had carefully arranged in the bottom of the basket.

Normally, when a box turtle was discovered, it was within close range of its nest where it would usually remain for life.

The Chief was surprised when he had learned that box turtles always stayed within two hundred yards of their nest and if someone picked one up and then later released it in the wild, it would most probably die.

How would he ever know where this unfortunate turtle had come from? He made a mental note to call the University of Wisconsin for advice.

A squad car was dispatched to the Pointing Dog Grocery. The on-duty officer in training had been told to purchase blueberries, or some other kind of fresh fruit, and a package of Oscar Mayer hotdogs for the turtle.

Since box turtles were omnivorous, Chief Smith planned to dig for earth worms in his front lawn after dark because the turtle would certainly prefer night crawlers to a sliver of a chemical-laden hotdog.

At least this latest prank only involves one slow-moving turtle, he thought. *I can handle this…*

Five years ago, he was called to the Mineral Point high school to remove thirty-five chickens from the parking lot, along with a large supply of chicken feed.

It had seemed then that every bird in Iowa County, except for the turkey vultures that roosted on top of the Point's water tower, had joined the chickens at their impromptu feast.

For years after the chicken incident, he was called, 'The Bird Man of Mineral Point.'

Even though he had worn thick gardening gloves and protective head gear, his hands still had a few permanent scars from being relentlessly pecked as he tried to capture and cage the hungry birds.

These senior class pranks had, until the last few years, been conducted in the spring, at the end of the school year.

Now, he never knew when to expect a senior class 'joke.'

The Chief was certain, however, that the scared-to-death, quivering students who had stampeded into the MP Police Station for protection that morning, were not the ones who had orchestrated the street theatre.

They were in shock upon arrival and he had called the local EMTs to the station to check the students' vital signs.

He would make it his top priority to flush out this year's guilty graduating seniors who had successfully disrupted so many lives today in Mineral Point—again.

This time, they had gone too far. The Chief was going to try to help everyone remain calm and focused and keep this incident under wraps as long as possible.

He had asked the students involved in the vampire incident that morning not to talk to anyone—even their parents, about what had happened.

He asked them to have their parents call him instead and he would try to answer their questions.

It was as if everyone believed that there really *was* a vampire, or at least something supernatural going on.

Now everyone was nervous and fearful, waiting for another vampire incident to unfold.

Even his mother, Margaret Smith, had called him after the incident had gone viral, to express concern and to ask him what he intended to do about 'things.'

Until today, he would never have thought his own mother could have been sucked into this melodrama.

He was hoping to have the whole thing resolved by tomorrow morning.

The Chief wondered how his mother had heard about the vampire incident. She did not live in a place that international news traveled to quickly.

She lived in Ireland, in the village of Rathreedane in the Townland of Bonniconlon, County Mayo.

MEDIKEA MOUND

For many years now, Sister Mary Agnes had prayed from sunrise to sunset, in the main chapel of the Medikea Mound Motherhouse.

Community vigils began at dawn in the Chapel of Saint Ann. Then there were late morning prayers at 10:00, followed by midday prayers, vespers and finally, compline, shortly before twilight each evening.

After sundown, she moved to the Reliquary Chapel and would spend the night there among hundreds of fragments of bones, individually encased behind glass. These were relics of holy men and women who had officially been declared Saints by the Catholic Church.

On the days when she was not actively engaged in spiritual warfare, there was a comfortable rhythm to her prayer life. She normally avoided the community meals with her fellow sisters each day because she was either not hungry or had forgotten to eat.

She kept to herself and prayed for people she did not know by name. People who were very much in need of spiritual protection or healing, whether they were aware of it or not.

Tonight, the setting sun had spread its rays lavishly over the main chapel, melting the reds and buttery yellows in the west wall's stained glass windows.

Like a newly formed stream of molten lava, the blended colors turned deep orange and flowed slowly over the pews.

When Sister Mary Agnes prayed here in the early morning, before communal prayers began, the chapel was often pierced by streaks of blinding white light, splattered with blotches of royal blue leaking in from the chapel's east wall windows. She enjoyed watching the blue spots dancing around on her white habit like she was looking into a kaleidoscope.

Mary Agnes was one of only a handful of nuns at the Motherhouse who had chosen to continue wearing the Order's traditional white habit.

She had never minded wearing the bulky, full-length robe and the long veil covering her short-cropped hair.

None of the sisters, with the exceptions of Sister Mary Agnes and Sister Mary Catherine, still chopped their own hair off.

Mary Agnes had noticed that since she had been aging, her hair did not seem to be growing as quickly as it had when she was a younger nun. She could no longer remember when it had been long enough to bother snipping it off.

When she needed to look in a mirror to adjust her veil or inspect her teeth, she could see that she was not showing obvious signs of aging. She always seemed to look the same.

There were never any new wrinkles or age spots or bags under Sister's tired eyes. This always surprised her because, since she got so little sleep, she thought she would look much worse. *Sleep is overrated*, she often said to herself.

She must be well over ninety now but she had the hands of a woman who was many decades younger— no knotted, bulging blue veins on her hands. No translucent skin.

Often in the distant past, when strangers walked into the convent unannounced, hoping to encounter a nun sitting in the entrance lounge to confide in and perhaps pray with them, Sister Mary Agnes was happy to comply.

She had sat there patiently, seven days a week, in between communal prayer in the Chapel of Saint Ann and her work in the convent library. Like a high-powered magnet, she attracted souls in need of spiritual assistance.

Over the years, the efficacy of Sister's prayers had become well known and people in need of spiritual help often came and asked for her specifically at the visitors' desk.

Medikea Mound became a destination place for retreats and pilgrims who traveled from far away states and often, foreign countries, just to meet with Sister Mary Agnes.

She had become known as a living saint. It was said by many that her sanctity allowed her to bi-locate like Saint Padre Pio had regularly done in the 1960's from his remote monastery in Italy.

There were several well documented accounts of Sister Mary Agnes being seen in two different places at the exact same time.

She had been identified in an Instagram, kneeling on the ground next to a young nun who had sustained life-threatening injuries from a mountain lion attack in Montana.

At the same time, she was seen praying over a hit and run victim in Los Angeles who had miraculously recovered from his injuries.

Sister Mary Agnes' face had been photographed at the scene of the accident, standing over a little boy who had been left for dead by an unidentified car.

The photo of her face was part of the evidence file that the accident investigators had collected at the site. Before they had been able to interview her, she had disappeared.

They had been able to locate her only because she had been wearing the habit of her religious order.

Because the investigators hoped that the nun had been an eye witness, they sent the photo to convents all over the world, hoping someone would know who she was.

A Sister of Saint Benedict in upstate New York had identified her, explaining that she had met Sister Mary

Agnes at a retreat long ago—and from looking at the photo, she had not aged at all since then.

When contacted by the authorities, Sister told the investigators that she did recall praying for a young boy once who had been left to die by a hit and run vehicle, but she had not seen it happen and she had no idea how she *could* have seen it take place because, as far as she knew, she had never been in Los Angeles.

When the weather permitted, Mary Agnes often sat outside the Motherhouse on an old wrought iron bench in between two tall ginkgo trees which had been planted there in the mid 1800's.

Occasionally, box turtles made their way across the patio, heading towards the small stream which ran along the back of the building.

Hundreds of years ago, there had been such an abundance of box turtles on the Mound that it had become known as 'Medikea' Mound—the Meskwaki Native American word for 'turtle.'

Near the top of the Mound, before the trail up became almost impassably steep, there was an ancient rock effigy of a turtle on a small, flat ledge.

Before her legs began to fail, Sister had regularly hiked up there to think and pray.

Even though it was not at the hill's summit, the views from the effigy ledge were heavenly. To the east were the rolling hills in the Driftless area of Wisconsin. To the west, the State of Iowa and the Mississippi River.

29

The Meskwakis called this area "Manitoumie"—the place where the Great Spirit loves to dwell.

Sister's extraordinary popularity with the visitors to the Motherhouse had not gone unnoticed by the other retired nuns.

Some of the younger ones, resented that they were never sought after. Especially since they considered themselves to be every bit as capable as Sister Mary Agnes, if not more so.

One day, completely out of the blue, under the pretense of saving Mary Agnes from the sin of pride, Mother Superior Mary Helen ordered her to no longer meet with people who came to the convent asking specifically for "Sister Mary Agnes."

"It would be prideful to think, Sister, that those who come here requesting only you, could not be helped by another sister."

"Perhaps our Sister Mary Dolorosa, who is many years younger than you, would be more suitable."

"Most importantly, she is also a trained counselor with a Master's Degree in Clinical Psychology."

"You must conserve your strength now, Sister, and spend your final years here at Medikea Mound in private prayer and contemplation."

After being ordered to stop helping people, she discovered the dark night of the soul.

She rarely spoke to others and no one ever said anything to her either. If she did try to strike up a conversation, she was ignored.

It somewhat confused Mary Agnes that even the politest sisters did not speak to her.

Ever.

The last conversation she remembered having, was when Mother Superior Mary Helen had ordered her to stop meeting and praying with people who came to the Mound to seek her help.

Gradually, Mary Agnes had stopped wondering why everyone snubbed her.

If the truth were known, she preferred remaining silent and keeping company with herself.

She rarely had any reserves left each morning, after spending most nights trying to comfort souls trapped in black holes throughout the universe.

After World War II, her world had inadvertently become a constant battle ground with Abaddon, in the realm of the fallen angels.

Mary Agnes often shook her head at the irony of only having two-sided conversations with people, if they were already dead.

The living no longer seemed to care if she came or went. Since Sister Mary Agnes had nowhere else to go at her age, she stayed on at Medikea.

It was never mentioned in the convent, that shortly after Mary Agnes had been forcibly 'retired,' pilgrims had stopped coming to Medikea Mound.

For several months, Mary Agnes watched from the shadows as disappointed people were turned away from the visitors desk, many of them in tears.

Sometimes, tears ran down her own face as she watched her old life passing by her in the lobby.

Occasionally, Sister Mary Dolorosa intervened and a visitor would sit with her in the lobby.

Mary Agnes was too far away to hear what they talked about but was relieved that Mary Dolorosa appeared to be a good listener.

Quite possibly, Mother Superior did the right thing by removing me...

A BALE OF TURTLES

If Susan was still fixated on the vampire street theatre, then Liffey would have to make it clear that she was more anxious to talk about the arrival of her friends—Sinéad, John and Luke, than she was to keep rehashing theories about what had taken place that morning at the bus stop.

The whole thing was childish. At least her brother Neil had been able to convince Robert Rivers to take him to the Chicago Zoo. Primary and middle school students had, like the high school students, been given the option to go home if a caregiver came to sign them out.

Even though Liffey too had been dismissed for the day, she had been loaded up with tons of homework and was also having some serious problems with her Hornpipe steps that she wanted to work on.

33

The zoo had been out of the question. Sometimes she wished her mother would stop trying to challenge her with more complex hard shoe steps.

Especially impossible Hornpipe steps.

Liffey had always hated doing the Hornpipe. It had been the most difficult dance for her to master. She always felt like *it* controlled her—not *vice versa.*

She *had* to dance well in Chicago in two weeks. She hoped this was because she was her mother's only student and she wanted to make her proud. But it was probably because she wanted to do at least as well as Sinéad.

Or maybe even better?

Liffey cringed when thoughts like these pointed out how very shallow she actually was. In spite of all her deep, daily Om meditating, she was still a competitive monster.

There were big plans that needed to be made to entertain her three soon-to-arrive guests. The only time John had been in Mineral Point before, there had been a freak blizzard and more drama than she cared to face again any time soon.

She knew that his twin brother was coming with him to prevent any more unexpected 'events.' He was obviously going to be their chaperone and Liffey could hardly fault his parents for their caution.

John had told Liffey that his mother said that she had almost fainted last year when she picked up the morning newspaper on their porch in New Hampshire and read the headline:

34

LOCAL HERO JOHN BERGMAN FOILS CURRENCY MELTDOWN!

When Mildred Bergman saw the front page photo of her son standing in front of a large helicopter with three unidentified men wearing FBI jackets, she did faint.

After that, she had become irrationally angry and said that he was never going to be permitted to go to visit *that Rivers girl* in Wisconsin ever again and to never, ever, even *think* about broaching that subject because the answer was always going to be: "No!"

Liffey had hoped that by now, John's family might have forgotten about that incident. It had been a whole year now and was ancient history.

Unfortunately, his parents also knew about a few of the unsettling events that had taken place during the Alaskan cruise where she had first met the Bergman family—like the Rivers family abandoning their rental car seconds before the car had exploded and the huge polar bear they had watched batting a man into the Arctic Ocean...

In retrospect, Liffey realized it was remarkable that Mildred Bergman had reluctantly given permission for John to visit Wisconsin again. With his brother.

I suppose they would prefer that their son had a tennis-player girlfriend who only worried about her next match and what she wore to school each day, Liffey sighed. *Sometimes I wish I were that girl too.*

Sinéad McGowan was coming to Chicago on the same day John Bergman and his brother Luke would also arrive at O'Hare Airport from New Hampshire.

Since Sinéad had already met the Bergmans on The Alaskan Sun cruise ship last year, the four of them could just pick up where they had left off. Also, it would be nice to be able to talk about the vampire incident with them and get their take on it. She needed some 'outside of Mineral Point' perspective.

Even though Liffey and John usually called each other several times a week, she missed him. It had now been almost a year since he had come to Mineral Point to help Aunt Jean move into her new house and they still talked about the almost unbelievable series of events they had shared during that visit. It was hard to believe that it had all happened.

Over the past year, she had come to realize that John's friendship made her like herself more. And he always made her laugh at his lame Knock Knock jokes. No matter *how* pathetic they were. He even laughed at her own pathetic Knock Knock jokes.

It was long past time for a real visit—no more Liffey Rivers dramas. Just normal, regular stuff.

Liffey was no longer sure that she knew what 'normal regular stuff' was anymore. Ever since St. Louis, her life had been as far away from normal as a total eclipse of the sun.

She had obviously failed to get permission to host a welcoming party for her friends in the safe house her father had built. It was meant to be a place where the Rivers family could safely hide and 'disappear'—if it came to that. So far, it had only been used once, when family friends had to seek shelter and disappear after a dangerous situation had developed which had soon threatened the Rivers as well.

When Robert Rivers had designed and then built the house underground, Liffey thought for sure that he had lost his mind and blamed herself. She knew next to nothing about it and neither of her parents would discuss why they thought it was suddenly so important to build such a fortress.

Unless…

Unless the man who had ruined her life, ever since she had inadvertently thwarted his conflict diamond smuggling ring in St. Louis at the Celtic Arch Feis ,was still 'out there' somewhere.

Unless…

Unless her parents feared that this man was going to surface again, because *maybe* he had not drowned in the Arctic Ocean after all?

Liffey had been told by the Interpol agents, who had helped her family several times, that she and her mother, Maeve, were probably the only people on earth who could make a positive ID of the so-called 'human being' that Liffey had nicknamed—Skunk Man.

The man who had supervised the most successful blood diamond smuggling operation in the world for many years.

The man who had helped several small countries in Africa finance revolutions which had created mass

37

destruction and brought death to hundreds or maybe even thousands of innocent people.

Liffey tried unsuccessfully to put these depressing, terrifying thoughts out of her mind as she ran into the house and upstairs to her room.

She quickly located her backpack and found the books she would need to do her homework later. Then she went to her parents' bedroom to look for Maeve's amazing camera so she could take some good close-ups of her new reptilian friends.

She found the camera on her mother's organized bookshelves and went out on her parents' balcony that overlooked the woods in back of the house.

As she panned the landscape with the camera's zoom features, she could hardly believe that she spotted two more box turtles walking out from the bigleaf ligularia plants and inching their way across the yard.

She watched incredulously as they stopped directly behind the other two turtles and looked up.

Now there were *four* motionless, endangered box turtles gawking up at the ginkgo trees!

Box turtles are supposed to be vanishing, but now there are four box turtles visiting ginkgo trees in my backyard?

Before Liffey could process this unlikely turtle convention, she slapped her mouth shut with her left hand to muffle her scream: "Noooooo WAY!"

She had never noticed this before, but looking out and down from her parents' balcony, trying to get good photos of the turtles at the far end of their yard, she could see that the field stones her mother had decided not to remove because they would make an excellent border for her plants, were arranged in the perfect outline of a *turtle!* Head, shell, four short legs and tail.

It *had* to be some kind of Native American animal effigy like the ones she had studied last year in her history of southwestern Wisconsin class.

Ever since she had learned about effigies, she had kept her eyes open when she drove around with her parents on their forced Sunday afternoon expeditions into the countryside, her brother constantly using his binoculars looking for black bears that never appeared and her parents looking for who knew what.

She had made the best of these outings ever since she was determined to find an effigy. She had seen a few earthen mounds in the fields across from an old Welsh church out in the middle of nowhere, but what she had really wanted to see, was exactly what she was now looking at in her own yard.

She knew that animal effigies were thought to mark places where religious ceremonies took place and were sometimes burial sites too. Were Native Americans buried under this effigy?

It was amazing that Maeve must have somehow known that she needed to leave the field stones right where they were and not rearrange them, Liffey thought.

Liffey was beginning to feel overwhelmed by all of the unexpected occurrences today—ground vibrating underneath her again, a howling coyote, a floating nun above the ginkgo trees and now four endangered box turtles visiting with those ginkgo trees?

She felt like a new Alice in a Wonderland, living in a world where nothing made sense. She made a mental note not to follow a white rabbit if one turned up. She was not going to fall down a hole before her friends got here.

She could hardly wait to show them a real Native American effigy in her own backyard!

Most effigies in this part of Wisconsin were dirt mounds in the shape of animals, like birds or snakes, turtles and bears. But some effigies, like the one in her backyard, were made with rocks that were arranged in animal shapes.

These were considered to be totems of the tribes—divine guardians with the power to protect the home of the tribe that had erected it.

Liffey felt giddy and weak with this discovery. She was not sure how much new information she could handle. Only this was not new. This effigy would have been here in her yard for at least a thousand years and possibly much longer.

I need figgy hobbin, NOW! Liffey thought anxiously.

After taking twenty photos of the newly discovered turtle effigy and then many more of the four box turtles, with their long, extended necks gawking at the ginkgo trees, she switched to video record.

I really should let little brother know about these turtles which must be living inside the rock effigy, except Neil might not be able to resist picking one up and that was illegal.

It would be foolish to have a juvenile crime record just because he picked up a turtle in his own backyard.

KOI

Before Liffey met up with Susan Scott at the Red Rooster, she decided to check up on her Aunt Jean, who now lived only two blocks away. She knew that her aunt would be interested in the box turtles.

Worried that if she told her aunt about the effigy, she might unintentionally encourage Aunt Jean to set up camp indefinitely beside it until something else distracted her, Liffey decided to just stick with the turtle report and leave the rock turtle effigy out of it.

For many years, ever since she had been in her aunt's 'School of Life,' Liffey had made it a point to nurture her aunt's interest in the animal world if she came across something unusual.

41

Animals were far more interesting than the people in the reality shows her aunt was now watching.

Aunt Jean was always obsessed with something and Liffey was glad that it was no longer Irish dancing that kept her aunt preoccupied.

At first, Aunt Jean's passion for Irish dance had been great because all Liffey had to do was mention a feis—no matter where it was, and her aunt was thrilled to take her.

The problem was, Aunt Jean was competing as an adult Irish dancer at the same competitions and Liffey had to constantly tell her what a great dancer she was and if things did not go well for Aunt Jean, Liffey had to console her for weeks afterwards.

It had been totally exhausting traveling around with her aunt, feis after feis, listening to how it was only a matter of time until she would be replacing the bad girl dancer in Lord of the Dance. Aunt Jean refused to believe that being a beginner Irish dancer at the age of forty was an obstacle and that it was not likely she was going to be the next Irish dancer chosen to star in a Michael Flatley show.

After a concerned doctor at a feis in New York had diagnosed her aunt with the worst case of "Post Traumatic Bling Syndrome he had ever seen," Jean Rivers had been cautioned not to watch bling-heavy entertainment.

He had emphatically ordered her aunt to avoid Swarovski crystals in general but especially *never* to look directly at a solo dress which had already been smothered with them, as it might cause a PTBD flare-up.

Until New York, Liffey had never heard of a Post Traumatic Bling Disorder. From what the doctor had said, her aunt must have a fairly serious condition.

The feis doctor in New York had also urged her aunt not to fake tan herself at feiseanna because it could contribute to her very precarious PTBS state of mind.

However, for the past eight months, Aunt Jean had completely lost interest in Irish dancing and had instead, turned her attention to koi fish and haiku.

So maybe I am just being paranoid about Aunt Jean's putting up a tent next to the turtle effigy, Liffey thought. *Besides, she is afraid of bugs.*

Liffey found her aunt sitting in her backyard on a slightly elevated redwood deck, gazing reflectively into the fish pond she had recently designed and installed.

After the water and filtering system lines were in place, she had stocked it with ten koi fish and planted exotic water plants on manmade steps, beginning twelve inches under water, to deter deer from being able to eat the plants while standing at the side of the pond.

Liffey sat down alongside her aunt, admiring the shimmering purplish-red fish scales gliding by her. It only took a moment for Liffey to see that the koi fish were the same magenta color as the yoga mat her aunt had just given her.

43

"However did you manage to get so many color-coded koi fish with the exact same magenta tone, Aunt Jean?" Liffey asked, genuinely interested.

There was a long silence and Liffey waited patiently for her aunt to collect her thoughts before answering the question. If she did answer it. Aunt Jean often just ignored a direct inquiry, like she was hard of hearing.

"I too have noticed that Mother Nature has been very generous to these lovely koi fish, Liffey," Aunt Jean replied, evasively. "In fact, I have been inspired to write about them in my haiku."

Aunt Jean then surprised Liffey with some very strange, even for her aunt, comments about koi fish in general:

"I have been reflecting upon what life might be like for these koi fish, long after I am gone and they are a few hundred years old."

Liffey raised her eyebrows.

"They can live to be two hundred years old, Liffey. Especially when someone like myself has been feeding them only gourmet fish food and has housed them in a large fish tank inside the house during our brutal Wisconsin winters."

"Just like smart humans who, like birds, will go to warmer climates to avoid harsh weather, I will have 'snow fish' which will add many years to their fishy lives." Liffey tried not to wince at her aunt's choice of the word, "fishy."

When Liffey had pointed out that, like the kind of parrots which would often out-live their owners, these koi fish, should her aunt successfully raise them to a very old age, might need some kind of fish society to take charge of them and move them elsewhere, her aunt had replied:

"Liffey darling, I am certain that I shall live to be very, very old. Remember back in Johannesburg, the day before the feis, when we consulted with that wise old Sangoma woman?"

"Yes I certainly do, Aunt Jean." *HOW could anyone have forgotten that wrinkled, ancient woman who had scattered a few pebbles on the ground and then told Liffey that she and the brother that she did not yet know existed, were both in the "shadow of the serpent?"*

"Well, darling, while you were sniffing exotic oils and investigating amulets, I went back to her and asked if she would scatter her little rocks again to determine how old I would be when I die."

"Aunt Jean," Liffey said irritably, "even if she *could* tell you such a thing, which she never would have because nobody can just tell someone when they are going to die, why would you have even asked such a question?"

Aunt Jean smiled benevolently and chose not to answer this question.

It had never ceased to amaze Liffey that her strange aunt could look like a wise old soul whenever she wanted to, because she had learned when to keep her mouth shut and just smile.

Liffey wished she were able to keep her own big mouth shut more often and just smile. It would probably make her complicated life a good bit easier.

Aunt Jean had recently become a devoted follower of Bashō, the famous Japanese Haiku poet who lived in the 1600's. Like Bashō, Aunt Jean had begun to write haiku poems.

While composing, she wore a shiny pink kimono sprinkled with delicate white cherry blossoms and scribbled her haiku on sheets of expensive rice paper, imported from Japan. For inspiration, Jean sipped cherry blossom tea from delicate Japanese teacups without handles.

Liffey had been trying hard to understand and empathize with her aunt during this manic haiku phase, but had recently become convinced that her aunt was simply flipping out again.

Today, Aunt Jean recited one of her favorite cat haiku poems by Hanato Fuki, a poet who, like her Aunt Jean, had also followed Basho:

I have swallowed fur
Shed by all the summer cats
I am so thirsty

When Liffey saw tears streaming down her aunt's face, she knew it was definitely time to alert her father about Aunt Jean's new haiku mania before things got totally out of control.

A cat shedding its fur each season when the climate warms up should NOT be a topic that would bring anyone to tears! Liffey thought.

This haiku thing would have been fine with Liffey if her Aunt Jean had just stayed *at home* in her pretty satin robe while she composed her haiku and sipped cherry blossom tea, but her aunt insisted on wearing the kimono when she attended the public gatherings of local haiku poets.

While Liffey was fairly certain that that the Mineral Point haiku community was charitable enough not to dismiss her strange aunt, Liffey knew that Aunt Jean looked ridiculous.

But then, so what? Liffey mused. *Who cares?* Since she had begun meditating, nothing really bothered her much anymore. Even her aunt's erratic behavior.

And after listening to her aunt recite another cat haiku by Hanato,

Lithe cat chases light,
Tries to catch pond reflections.
Koi oblivious,

Liffey was somewhat relieved. At least now she knew where her aunt had gotten the idea for what had seemed like an out-of-the-blue, crackpot idea—the new koi fish pond.

She actually liked the Hanato haiku with its image of the lithe cat swiping at its own reflection in a pond.

47

Liffey hoped that her Aunt Jean knew better than to get a 'lithe cat' though, because if she did get that cat, her koi fish were likely not going to be living very long lives after all.

A memory of howling suddenly assaulted Liffey's head. She was almost sure she had heard a coyote howling earlier that day. She doubted she had been dreaming then. Coyotes were cats. Would Aunt Jean be attracting coyotes to feast at her pond?

The mysterious new haiku poet had worn sunglasses again to the haiku reading held last Saturday morning, even though it had been a dismal, overcast day. He told the regular haiku authors that he had an allergy to sunlight and was being extra-cautious, as one never knew when the sun was going to pop out from behind protective cloud cover.

He knew that he was going to have to listen to discussions and recitation of haiku for at least twenty minutes before he would be able to escape without creating a bad impression.

This would be his third and last get-together with these haiku poets. He was not even sure what a haiku was but as the ruthless real estate world had always proclaimed: "Location! Location! Location!"

The man counted eight people present, including Liffey Rivers' ding bat aunt who was wearing a shiny bathrobe.

He pretended to appreciate the warm welcome the poets extended and adlibbed how he was honored to be with such an illustrious group.

48

His glue-on moustache itched terribly and he had to concentrate hard not to rip it off his face.

Clip-on, fake pierced hoop earrings, were digging into his earlobes like they were determined to bore permanent holes.

Worst of all, he was sweating, which made him fear that the gray highlights he had combed into his thick black hair were going to melt and run down his neck. He should have worn one of his wigs.

After he politely listened to three poets read their recent haiku, he could no longer take it. He explained that he had to leave because he had suddenly become ill.

Which was partially true. The stress caused by his thrown together disguise was making him queasy.

Promising to be back for their next meeting, he quickly exited The Foundry Books through the door leading to the parking lot on the south side of the building.

Slowly, he began his grounds inspection, greatly relieved that, just as he had anticipated, no one had followed him. People normally stayed far away from one another if someone said they were sick, because they might be contagious.

Studying his tunnel notes, he picked up his pace and walked gingerly along the west side of the building.

"Eureka!" he called out softly when he found what he had been looking for—the entrance to an old abandoned mine, now filled in to keep children and tourists out.

It was still there, right in back of the building on the side of a small hill.

Location! Location! Location!

This is almost too good to be true, he thought.

He made a mental note to send the haiku group a box of expensive chocolates and ten bottles of South African wine from one of the vineyards he owned— after this was over.

It would not be long now.

AN OLD SOUL

Aunt Jean suddenly sprang up from her deck chair, closed her eyes and jumped into a lunge position. She often did this right in the middle of a conversation. Like she was in some kind of *en garde* sword duel but without the sword. Or an opponent.

She then began humming, slowly raising the sound level until she sounded like a bee hive—like propellers might sprout out from her ears and she would soon start flying around the pond like a winged insect.

The buzzing "Ommm..." noise her aunt was making and the fact that her eyes were still closed, provided sufficient cover for Liffey to sneak away without having to explain why she could not stay for an extended visit.

Aunt Jean sometimes held this lunge position for twenty minutes or so, explaining to Liffey afterwards that she was "an old soul."

Whatever that was supposed to mean. *She might still be in this position when I get back from figgy hobbining,* Liffey thought.

Liffey tiptoed away from the pond, contemplating whether or not her 'old-soul' aunt might think that this high gate could actually keep fish predators such as blue herons and raccoons away from her fish pond. The gate was high—the fence, not so high.

It would not surprise her if Aunt Jean *did* think the low fence and high gate would keep blue herons and raccoons and lithe cats away from her fish. *Like birds seriously have to open gates to gain access to backyard ponds to look for fish and raccoons, and cats don't know how to climb over fences?*

Aunt Jean often analyzed her surroundings like a two-year-old might see things.

It was hard to take her aunt seriously. However, as Liffey stepped up her pace, so as not to keep Susan waiting at the Red Rooster, something her aunt had said recently continued to bother her.

After normal chit-chat exchanges having lunch together last week, Aunt Jean's face clouded over and she blurted out: "Liffey I must tell you that I am tired of thinking about Sheng Fui! I am now concentrating only on the 'Ma' of things."

Liffey had no idea what her aunt was talking about, but listened politely to see if Aunt Jean would reveal more. It often took several minutes to unscramble her aunt's run-on thought patterns.

"I am learning to honor empty space, Liffey. The 'Ma.' I can think more clearly when I have little or nothing surrounding me. But I must tell you, there is something strange and alarming going on now, right here in our Mineral Point. Everything smells rotten. Something sinister and dangerous is in our midst now and I do not like it one bit."

"It is like being in the vicinity of a zoo with vague animal smells wafting through the air. My skin often feels like something is crawling on it—like little bugs are running up and down my arms and legs and sometimes, even all of me."

"I think that there is an infestation going on here in the Point, Liffey. And as much as it pains me to say this, I think that the infestation started within my haiku group of poets."

"Do you mean like an infestation of bedbugs or fleas?"

"No, Liffey. I am talking about an infestation of evil. A kind of bad energy infestation."

Liffey suddenly became very interested in this peculiar observation made by her peculiar aunt so off-handedly.

"Let me explain. When I first joined the Haiku group, there was an airy, good feeling. However, things have changed. We have a new member and to be quite honest, I do not like him at all. He frightens me."

53

"Are you saying that you actually think that one of your haiku poets is sinister, Aunt Jean?" This was hard to believe.

Aunt Jean replied immediately: "Yes, I am, Liffey. Someone is 'off.' I am certain of it."

"Do you know which one of them it is, Aunt Jean?" Liffey asked, hesitant to broach such a delicate subject.

"Yes, I think I do. It's a new man who said he had just moved to Mineral Point. I only saw him three times. Then he just disappeared. No one else has seen him either."

"He seemed nice at first, but I am telling you, Liffey, he is the cause of the infestation. I know it. He showed up out of nowhere and now that he is gone, there is a smell of decay everywhere. Like rotten meat or eggs gone bad. Have you not noticed it here in my backyard?"

Liffey actually *had* noticed a subtle change in the air quality all over Mineral Point but how in the world could one man be blamed for that kind of thing?

"It must be air pollution coming here from smelly factories—maybe even all the way from Chicago when there are certain wind currents. Our backyard smells funny too, Aunt Jean. "

Putting the unsettling conversation with her aunt out of her mind for the time being, Liffey stepped up her pace.

She wondered if Susan Scott had more information by now about whatever it was that had happened that morning at the bus stop.

Susan knew almost everyone at the small local high school. If there had been some significant updates, Susan would definitely know.

One thing that bothered Liffey a lot about everyone seeming to think that it was this year's senior class prank, was that *none* of the students involved so far were seniors.

There had been two freshmen, three sophomores and one junior.

No seniors.

She thought that this would not only be highly unusual, but it would just NEVER happen. *Senior class pranks are organized by and for seniors and involve only seniors,* Liffey thought. Those underclassmen were not part of whatever it was that had happened.

They were victims.

So who were those actors?

Liffey also thought that each of the actors in the well-planned morning vampire skit had to have been professionals. It was not possible for students to have enacted a complicated skit with sophisticated special effects so successfully.

Liffey had seen the school play last year and it did not have a cast of polished actors. It was amateurish. Apparently the vampire drama was not.

Was it just some kind of bizarre 'street theatre' they had been performing for some reason? Their skit had had a major effect on, not only all the students in Mineral Point, but also the teachers, school staff and by now, probably the entire State of Wisconsin.

Downtown was almost deserted. As she passed the **CLOSED** sign in front of the Gray Dog, she recalled the conversation she had last November with Susan at the Red Rooster when her friend had told her about the 'vampire' that had surfaced long ago in Mineral Point.

Susan had said that sometimes it had been seen in a cemetery. Other times, in residential areas, when it would jump down from a tree branch and give chase to terrified passersby.

Another time the vampire had supposedly popped up from underneath a private dock at Lake Ludden where two teenagers were fishing at dusk. They had been chased by the creature all the way back to their parked car.

Liffey tried not to think about how terrifying, yet thrilling, it would be if there really *was* a vampire lurking under the ground, living in an abandoned mine shaft far beneath the city.

Apparently no one had ever owned up to being the town ghoul and it had not happened again.

Until maybe now?

However, today had apparently not featured the vampire wearing a long black cape and chasing people. There had supposedly been an emaciated old man, a puff of black smoke that might have *looked* like a vampire's cape and a blast of frigid air.

Since the students who witnessed the event had all run away, who really knew if there actually had been a cape?

Vampire or not, Liffey was fairly certain that she would never have run off like those students had this morning. At least she liked to think so.

I would have hidden somewhere close by to observe. And, come on! Not ONE of those witnesses thought to take a photo or make a video? Really? They could have documented the whole thing on their mobile phones and this mystery would be solved by now.

Apparently, there had been no one on the scene, other than the students. And they had been so terrified during the ordeal, that it had quickly become apparent that none of them were going to be able to help Chief Smith with some solid observations to help him figure out what had actually taken place.

Or at least enable him to come up with some kind of a logical explanation for what had happened.

The 'event' had been described by the witnesses, as comparable to watching a horror movie—but off the screen. As if whatever was really going on was not being done just for the students who were waiting at the bus stop.

Susan Scott was the only customer in the Red Rooster and she was trying not to eat all of her figgy hobbin before Liffey Rivers arrived—whenever that might be. If she were to be candid with herself, she would have to admit that it *really* annoyed her when Liffey was late and Liffey was almost always at least ten minutes late for everything.

This would be understandable if they lived in a bigger city where public transportation could often cause delays. But here in Mineral Point? Walking was the only method of getting around in the Point for the under sixteen, non-licensed drivers.

Liffey needed to learn how to time things so that she was not always late. At school, Susan often watched Liffey hugging the hall walls in the morning, trying to be invisible after the final buzzer.

Liffey had tried to explain how she could not help being late because she was 100% Irish and it was not in her genetic makeup to be prompt.

Susan marveled how it obviously did not appear to bother Liffey much—if at all.

Well, I'm part Irish too and it DOES bother me, Susan thought. She picked up her backpack and stomped out of the café. She decided to ignore the texts she was sure to receive later from Liffey as well.

She had her own friends here and certainly did not need a new one. Being friends with Liffey Rivers really did not matter much and she was tired of putting up with her. *Even though she did find our family's gold mine.*

So, from now on, Susan decided, *I won't put up with her. I am moving on….*

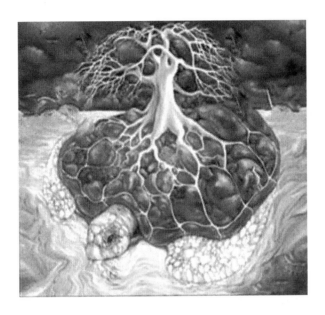

MYTH

He had spent several hours familiarizing himself with the popularity of the Wendigo myth featured in video games, horror movies and comic books. The more the Chief discovered, the more perplexed he became. This Wendigo hoax was far more complicated than he had realized at first.

He was now very relieved that the students had not seen the poem left inside the little haiku house this morning. If they *had* read it, they might have believed that this evil, mythological creature, had come to life. Fortunately, only himself and Officer Patterson had read the confusing prose and he had taken the extra precaution of locking it in his evidence safe.

At first, he had thought that the Wendigo creature had been created by Marvel Comics or perhaps video game developers. Discovering that the movies and games were based on a real Native American myth had been a total surprise. An unwelcome surprise.

Digging deeper, he learned that the Wendigo was an Iroquois Nation legend about a monster that was always famished. It had once been a human being but had become a cannibal to satisfy its insatiable hunger. Its hunger could never be satiated and a Wendigo grew taller after each person it devoured.

Chief Smith was completely taken aback when he discovered that there had been several murder trials in the early 1900's in which men were charged with brutally killing someone because they were sure that the person they murdered was turning into a Wendigo.

The Wendigo legend, according to the Meskwaki, was a demonic spirit which could be over fifteen feet tall. Its eyes glowed. It had a long tongue and yellow fangs. Its sallow skin exuded a disgusting odor of rotten meat. They were called 'Skin Walkers' by the Native Americans because they were so skinny, they appeared to be one-dimensional.

Selfish people who had become overpowered by greed were most at risk for turning into a Wendigo— or so the story went.

The Wendigo sometimes appeared as a monster with some characteristics of a human. Other times, it was a spirit who had actually possessed human beings and made them become monstrous cannibals.

He was uncertain whether or not he should release the frightening haiku poem. He thought it would be wiser to wait until the sensationalism died down.

The box turtle part of his investigation was basically leading nowhere. He had learned that many creation stories among the Native Americans in southwestern Wisconsin, embraced the legend that the earth had been created on the back of a turtle.

However, he could not imagine how that gentle tale would be relevant to a Wendigo scare in Mineral Point.

He had also come across some unpleasant turtle stories. Particularly the one about how in Greece, turtles were thought by many to be messengers from hell.

So. I am supposed to figure out how a turtle, a flesh-eating Wendigo, who apparently is also a poet who composes haiku poems, a horrific odor and what I think is some kind of Japanese word on a turtle's shell are somehow all tied together?

It occurred to Chief Smith, that perhaps he should never have gotten out of bed that morning.

After deciding to take a break from turtles, he scanned the page that had the computer-generated symbols and copied and pasted them on a 'Japanese to English' online translator.

If they were not Japanese, he would try Chinese, then Korean and so on. Since these characters were the ones used in the haiku found in the box, the Chief was almost certain they were Japanese, as he knew that is where the haiku tradition had started.

61

A few seconds later, the Mineral Point Chief of Police could not suppress the profound sense of dread surging through him when the Japanese-to-English translation appeared on his computer screen:

復讐 ＝ Revenge

Suddenly, the box turtle made sense. Why had he not immediately connected these symbols with the turtle? He saw clearly now that the pattern on the turtle's shell was exactly the same as the one on the copy paper.

They matched perfectly.

Had what he thought up until now, had only been this year's senior class prank, just been confirmed to be some kind of vendetta threat? His mind raced. *In ancient Greece, my research told me, turtles were thought by many to be messengers from hell...*

He reluctantly speed dialed the number an Interpol agent had programmed into his phone last November as that agency was leaving Mineral Point. The Interpol agent had asked him to, "Call this number immediately if anything happens here that could be interpreted as an out-of-the-ordinary threat—even if you have no idea what that threat might concern."

A voice message answered the Chief's call:

"You have reached Agent Paul Farley. Please leave a message."

FROM BAD TO WORSE

On-duty today for the first time by himself, deputy trainee Tony Patterson chatted amicably with the part-time cashier as she scanned a small package of bruised, out of season blueberries and an Oscar Mayer hot dog eight pack.

It was 10:00 a.m.

When she commented about how she had never seen him buying blueberries before and hoped that he had begun to realize how important fresh fruit was for a healthy lifestyle, he had answered:

"Well, I wish these were for me but they're for the box turtle the Chief found inside the haiku box this morning at The Foundry Books."

When the interested cashier quizzed the new policeman about whether or not he thought there was anything to the vampire rumor that was all over town, Officer Patterson continued feeding her the facts like the inexperienced law enforcement officer he was proving himself to be.

"Yep. It was all very unpleasant. That poor little turtle was inside that stuffy poem box with some lame poem about a Wendigo and a piece of paper with Japanese words."

"Let me see now, I think I've got the haiku poem memorized. This is just between you and me, right?"

The cashier nodded and said, "Of course, Officer!"

Wearing a smirk on his soft young face, he folded his hands dramatically and began to recite the haiku in a melodramatic, sing-song high-pitched voice:

"Trees are whispering.
Darkness erases the sun.
When Wendigo comes."

The deputy rolled his big green eyes, shook his blonde head, and strutted out of the store with his hotdogs and blueberries.

He turned back to flash a charming smile and little goodbye wave at the friendly cashier, savoring his first day on active police duty.

He rocked.

She had called him, "Officer."

As soon as the excited cashier saw the police car leaving Pointing Dog's parking lot, she immediately called her daughter Anne, who had been sent home

64

from high school classes, and told her what the officer had personally confided to her.

She told her daughter she would be home soon and not to tell anyone about what the officer had told her "confidentially," because it might cause trouble.

She repeated that she had promised the nice young new officer she would not tell anyone about what he had "confidentially," told only her. However, she did not consider her daughter to be untrustworthy with regard to keeping her mouth shut.

Anne hardly ever even talks to me anymore now that she's so busy with studying and cheerleader practices. And I'm her mother. If she doesn't talk to me anymore, why on earth would she talk to anyone else about this?

After she had asked Anne what a Wendigo was, the cashier's face had flushed deep pink with excitement and she immediately called her friend Maggie, who could be relied upon to keep her mouth shut. Maggie immediately called her son, Richard, who texted his friend Jack, who texted his cousin Shane, who called his mom at the utility company, which by then had already activated their volunteer emergency task force for an emergency meeting.

Anne Pembroke, having been only the second person after her mother to learn about the Wendigo from the police, immediately called her boyfriend and asked him to come over. She was afraid to be alone.

Then she texted all of her contacts, warning them to "beware" and to "take cover somewhere safe, "Immediately!"

This impromptu phone tree continued for hours. By noon, there were over eighty thousand posts on Facebook warning everyone in the vicinity of Mineral Point, Wisconsin, to use "extreme caution."

At 11:15 a.m., television and radio stations began to broadcast a: **Mineral Point Vampire Rises Again** headline.

By 2:00 p.m., all of Iowa County was talking in hushed tones about the wolfman or vampire or Big Foot or the Beast of Bray Road--whatever it was, that was on the loose.

Most of the locals had secured themselves in their homes after vampire-proofing their premises and were treating it like the 'Warning' category for a tornado that had been sighted nearby.

Without authorization or cause, the tornado sirens to take shelter immediately, were activated off and on all morning, throughout Iowa and Grant counties, by unauthorized parties.

There was talk of sending the National Guard to Mineral Point.

By 3:00 p.m. all of southwestern Wisconsin was on alert and the six students who had experienced the frightening event were doing personal interviews, skyping with newscasters from all over the world.

They had suddenly become famous.

When Adele Smith, the Chief's wife, had called expressing concern, he assured her it was all very hush-hush and would remain so until his forensic experts had tested some paper and ink—and released their results—if they chose to do so.

66

He did not tell his wife that he feared the worst and that he had already called in the Feds. Interpol had ordered him to speak only with them and, in case of an unforeseen emergency, his staff.

When he asked Adele not to discuss what had happened that morning, she suppressed a groan and promised to keep it all to herself—not to tell anyone. She hoped that maybe he was kidding. He admitted that he was a tad bit concerned that he had begun to receive inquiries and requests for his 'statement' but his dispatcher was on top of things.

Is my husband really that clueless? I can certainly keep my promise not to tell anyone since apparently the entire universe already knows by now, she sighed. *Who could I possibly tell that doesn't already know every single detail?*

John Bergman, and his twin brother, Luke, were doing damage control. They assured their overly protective, anxious mother, that Liffey Rivers had had nothing to do with the stupid Wendigo senior class prank in Mineral Point.

Liffey had thought it had been childish and very inconsiderate—as did they of course.

She was going to meet them at the airport in one of her father's law firm limos. It would get Liffey up in Mineral Point and then backtrack to Chicago to pick them up at O'Hare. Then the limo would drive everybody immediately back up to Wisconsin.

Knowing that his mother could never have enough 'factual information' to be completely satisfied, John went on: "Liffey's friend Sinéad McGowan's flight from Dublin is scheduled to arrive two hours before us. So she would have time to get to our terminal's baggage area where we will all wait together outside for Liffey and the limo."

When John detected that his mother still seemed to be having second thoughts about his upcoming visit to Wisconsin, he assured her that there would only be the chauffeured limo involved. And they would stand at least two feet back from the curb while waiting. No public transportation would be involved. Just the safe limo with its professional driver.

They would drive directly to the Rivers' house in Mineral Point and stay away from any senior high school students who might have been involved in the Wendigo joke.

Since both he and his brother were, like Liffey, only sophomores, there was zero chance any of the older students would want them around anyway.

They would be staying in the Rivers' real house—not the safe house, since it was still being investigated. Maeve Rivers and Liffey's father, Robert Rivers, would make sure nothing happened again.

"What happened in Mineral Point last year had been totally random," John tried to explain.

"Like when that flying eagle dropped that big turtle on that playwright Aeschylus's head over a thousand years ago while he was walking on the beach. That too, of course, had been totally random. Naturally, that had never happened again to the famous Greek tragedy playwright, because it had regrettably, killed him, but the point is, nothing bad is going to happen visiting Liffey Rivers and her family this time."

Luke Bergman shook his head disgustedly. What was wrong with his brother? *Like his little speech about a dead Greek who lived thousands of years ago is going to calm Mildred down? Now she'll worry about things falling from the sky!*

John picked up on Luke's cues and tried to improve his monologue: "Our only out of town excursion is going to be an Irish dance competition in Chicago where Liffey and her friend Sinéad will be competing and BOTH of Liffey's parents are going to supervise."

Finally, he assured his mother that Liffey's flaky Aunt Jean would not be in charge of the Chicago trip but he could not honestly say that she would not be tagging along.

Secretly, John hoped that a few private detectives would be tagging along, guarding Liffey, on the trip to Chicago. His life was below zero dull compared to hers.

He still grinned when he remembered solving the safe house's lock down problem. That had been better than winning his state tennis championship singles match last year.

Much better, because it had been obvious that Liffey had been very impressed with his ingenuity.

Sinéad McGowan tried unsuccessfully to convince her two older brothers, Eoin and Michael, that she would not need their police detective expertise in Wisconsin, just because there was supposed to be a bogus vampire scaring people where she was going.

"Sure. Right! Come on! Just like you did not need our help here in Sligo up on top of Knocknarea with that insane man on the black horse, or in Alaska with that same psychotic criminal who is always turning up, even though he is supposed to be dead?"

"We are coming with you Sinéad and that is final," Michael said.

Sinéad knew immediately that she did not stand a chance of convincing them otherwise and answered, "So then, where will you two doofuses be staying?"

"That is our little secret, little sister. We will keep a low profile and you will never see us. We have to come along, you know. Mam won't let you go back to the States without us. Your friend Liffey Rivers attracts trouble like ponds attract ducks."

"Both of your devoted and totally over-worked detective brothers needed a vacation anyway. Our drug busts in Dublin are becoming more and more problematic," Eoin confided.

"Anyway, our superiors thought it would be a good idea for us to get away for a bit before our cover is completely blown in Ireland," Michael agreed.

The Chief held his breath, hoping that the incoming fax was not going to make things worse than they already were.

It was the forensic report regarding the paper and ink which had been used to compose the Wendigo haiku.

He had been correct about the animal skin parchment—almost. The report said that the haiku poem had been written on parchment made from goatskin, not calves, as he had suspected.

The lab in Madison had traced it to the Afripaper Company which made parchment paper from animal skin and filled 'special orders.'

Afripaper was located in South Africa.

The ink used for writing the haiku was not blood. It consisted entirely of non-poisonous sumac berries. It too had been made in South Africa and was heavily marketed worldwide as an ink used for making paper crafts.

"Well, that's really helpful," the Chief grumbled to the box turtle that was chewing on a small sliver of an Oscar Mayer hot dog.

However, after he had faxed the information to Interpol, he had been amazed at how keyed up they were about what the Chief had thought was going to be pretty much dull, worthless information.

He was also surprised when Interpol told him that, based on the forensic report he had just forwarded, the box turtle was going to be air lifted in a matter of hours.

A small jet would land at Iowa County Airport and would need their 5,000 foot runway to land. The Chief was told that after he called the airport manager and made sure they were prepared for the Interpol jet, he needed to "secure the turtle."

71

The Chief was not in the mood to "secure the turtle." Whatever that meant? How much securing does a turtle need?

And how could his life get any more bizarre? Interpol said they would fax turtle-packing directions.

He called the airport and set up the landing time with the general manager. There was no control tower at the little airport but there would be a few mechanics working and the manager said he would be there to troubleshoot.

Interpol's written turtle directions were somewhat detailed. He needed two boxes and one of them must fit inside the other box. He should punch twenty small air holes in both boxes.

The turtle must be put in a pillowcase because it reduces the stress that the turtle would undergo if it could see what was happening. *Seriously?*

Put Styrofoam packing peanuts on the bottom of the smaller box and place the turtle in the box. Then pack more Styrofoam packing peanuts around it. Also, make sure that the peanuts are loose enough so air can flow through them, but try to make sure there are enough peanuts so that the turtle will not be able to move around.

Next put packing peanuts on the bottom of the bigger box and place the box with the turtle in it on top of them. Then put some more peanuts on either side of the turtle box and also above it and it is set to go.

POND TALK

Liffey had been waiting for Susan Scott at the Red Rooster for over twenty minutes before she texted her. It was not like Susan to be late. She had never before kept Liffey waiting. Liffey had to admit that it was always the other way around. She had, unintentionally, kept Susan waiting many times.

Something serious must have come up. She would try texting again later but wondered why Susan had not immediately replied.

73

It was very nice of Susan to have left me a piece of figgy hobbin, Liffey acknowledged, *but I am surprised she did not leave a note.*

Was she imagining things, or had Susan suddenly cooled off and was deliberately distancing herself?

Lately at school, it had been obvious that Susan had been avoiding her. Now her friend was sitting at the popular students' lunch table.

Liffey realized that Susan had known most of these people since kindergarten, so perhaps it had not been a mean girl, deliberate snub.

But every single day? And why hadn't Susan invited her to join her at that table this year? Like last year? Just once?

Now Liffey ate her lunch at the singles' table' with students like herself, who were not part of any clique. It had only taken her one lunch period to decide that she liked the singles' table much more than the other option.

The singles' table talked about what was going on outside in the real world. Not just school gossip. Liffey now regretted that during her freshman year, because she had been flattered by Susan's attention, she had let her new friend direct her social activities.

As Liffey slowly made her way back to her aunt's house, deep in thought, she continued to think about how Susan had been deliberately pretending not to see her in the school halls. *We have never had a serious argument or even a mild disagreement about anything that I can think of. And why is there a police car following me now?*

Before Liffey let herself in again through her aunt's six-foot-high, wrought iron gate, she stopped and surveyed the horrific changes that had taken place in the short time that she had been gone.

When she spied her aunt rushing towards her from the garden shed in a manic state of pure glee, Liffey tried to remain calm. It was obvious that her Aunt Jean was ready to explode with excitement.

"Aunt Jean, the fact that your backyard now looks like an animal decoy theme park is totally amazing. How in the world did you do all this work in the past hour?" Liffey asked, as her aunt opened the gate.

Aunt Jean smiled broadly. "While you were eating your hobbin pudding, darling, your father dropped your brother off for a visit and I put him to work unpacking the deliveries from yesterday. He is a good little worker. He's out in the shed now unpacking my owl."

So they are back from Chicago already? I wonder why? Daddy obviously changed his mind about the trip to the zoo...

Liffey tried not to visibly grimace as she took in the dramatic changes to her aunt's backyard. Beyond the pond, she spotted a plastic black bear peeking out from behind a cluster of leafless bushes. It had shiny plastic claws and menacing plastic eyes. Neil would love that.

There were also large signs *facing the woods:*

KEEP OUT
NO TRESPASSING

BEWARE OF DOG
NO ENTRY
HAZARDOUS ZONE

Did Aunt Jean think animals could read?

Upon closer inspection, Liffey could see three very plastic-looking yard deer looking out from the woods, a large raccoon decoy on a low-hanging tree branch and a life-like sandhill crane standing on the other side of the pond.

Suddenly Liffey got it. Except for the three deer, all of these peculiar decoys could be considered fish predators and would most definitely be interested in eating the koi in Aunt Jean's pond—if they were real. Her aunt must be trying to frighten fish-poaching animals away with rival decoy predators? So why the deer?

A foul odor wafted her way. Like her aunt had said, the backyard smelled "off." Other than the fact that it smelled disgusting, Liffey had no idea what it was. It reminded her of rotten meat.

"I bet Neil must think that your backyard is better than that safari boat ride at Disney, Aunt Jean," Liffey said, trying to muster some enthusiasm.

"We have only just begun to fortify my pond, darling. Within a very short time, your brother and I have come up with some amazing ideas. We are going to set timers and have dogs barking throughout the day. At night, we are going to alternate bears growling and coyotes howling."

"Good idea about the coyotes howling, Aunt Jean. Maybe you should also get a few coyote decoys? Make a pack of coyotes? I think I heard one behind our house today in the woods."

Trying to be polite, but mostly trying not to laugh, Liffey asked her aunt what else had to be done. *It's good that the nearest neighbor, other than her family, to this pond theme park, lives more than two blocks away,* Liffey thought, trying hard not to erupt into uncontrollable laughter and imagining how much fun it would be bringing her soon to arrive guests here for a tour.

"Well, for starters, I am not at all sure this sandhill crane decoy will keep a blue heron out of the yard. My blue heron decoy is on order and should arrive by tomorrow along with the snake and alligator decoys. There is a code of honor among blue herons, Liffey, that would not apply to a sandhill crane and a blue heron interacting."

Liffey put a serious look on her face and prepared herself, as best she could, for her aunt's heron lecture.

"If a blue heron is flying around looking for a pond to raid and there is already a blue heron on the premises raiding the same pond that the flying heron sees, the flying heron will not land and interfere with the blue heron that beat it to that pond."

"It will continue flying around looking for another opportunity to eat a fish. Perhaps it would stand in a shallow stream and wait for a trout to come swimming by. That is the code among all blue herons, Liffey. Not to directly interfere with another one of their own kind."

"Whereas, this sandhill crane decoy would have no influence as to deterring a heron raid. There could be a territorial bird fight for rights to my pond. "

"This could get ugly, Liffey," Aunt Jean finished, nervously running her fingers through her newly dyed, caramel brown hair.

Liffey was without words and nodded.

"Neil has agreed to move all the yard decoys to different positions each morning on his way to and from school to confuse any predators that might be studying this pond and waiting for an opportunity to attack my koi fish. I will pay him handsomely to keep my fish safe."

"Aunt Jean, I have only seen a few blue herons since we moved here and they were way on the other side of Madison. What makes you think there will be patrols of them flying over Mineral Point looking for fish?"

"And why would you need snakes and an alligator decoy? A Wisconsin heron may have seen an alligator or two on its winter migration route but would probably not recognize plastic alligators and pythons as being threats to them here in Wisconsin."

"What else have they got to think about, Liffey darling? They are just birds. They fly around all day looking for prey. All birds have bird brains, you know. There is not much room in their little heads for complicated behavior."

"Well, I intend to keep ahead of those flying fish predators. Neil has some brilliant ideas for the GBHs which we can act on immediately as well."

"GBHs?" Liffey asked.

"Yes, 'Lifsis.' That's what we call 'pond talk' for Great Blue Herons," Neil explained, over hearing the question as he deposited a duck decoy on the deck and headed back to the garden shed.

Liffey tried not to react when her brother called her "Lifsis." She hated that nickname but did not want to offend him because he thought it was very clever. And she certainly did not want to spoil his fish pond enthusiasm. His pond duties would keep him away from the box turtles and ginkgo trees at home.

"Just remember, Aunt Jean, he is only ten," Liffey said as her brother disappeared into the shed again.

"Why Liffey! I am surprised at your uppity, put-down attitude. Neil brings with him insights that only a ten-year-old child, who will soon be eleven, could think of. He sees the world through innocent eyes but at the same time, he realizes, thanks to violent video games, how dangerous this world can be!"

"Also, he has, thanks to his being a very bright child, figured out how to set up a dark screen to do holograms of Jurassic Park dinosaurs roaming about."

"His theory is that these projected dinosaurs will keep the dangerous, nocturnal predators at bay— along with the bears, howling dogs and coyote sound tracks."

"Sounds good to me, Aunt Jean. You and Neil seem to have covered all the koi fish predator bases."

Liffey was very grateful that Aunt Jean had turned to haiku writing and koi fish protection to keep busy, thinking again how nice it was that her aunt's dream of dancing the bad girl lead in Lord of the Dance had finally come to an end.

Aunt Jean would keep busy now with Pond Patrol.

Before Liffey could apologize for her display of insensitivity regarding her opinion of ten-year-old boys, Neil came out from the shed dragging a larger than life owl decoy behind him.

He was obviously thrilled to be involved in all this predator lunacy and Liffey resolved to treat both Neil and her aunt with more respect from this point on— difficult as it might be.

"Before you show me your new decoys, let me show you and Aunt Jean the pictures I took this morning of four box turtles in our own backyard!"

"This owl will also be one of my holograms," Neil said, ignoring his sister's invitation, "along with the dinosaurs I am designing. I think I will rotate them to keep the predators guessing."

Liffey smiled. Neil could be very disarming, but also a bit rude. He spoke four languages, so it was understandable that he missed being polite cues from time to time. It was very cute that he thought he could figure out how to make holograms to roam and fly around the property, protecting the pond.

Liffey handed Neil her mobile and told him to click on the Turtle Album in the pictures gallery.

Waiting for his reaction, Liffey studied her little brother's face.

It was blank.

Finally he said, "Liffey, there are no turtles here. Just pictures of our yard. No turtles. There's a squirrel in one of the ginkgo trees, but that's all."

"Where are the turtles?"

Liffey chimed in, agitated. "That's impossible Neil, I took a zillion turtle photos. First the two box turtles, and then lots more of all four when two more turtles showed up."

"Did you delete them by mistake?" Neil asked gently. Liffey did not answer his question.

Something must have malfunctioned. Fortunately, she had used her mother's camera when she took lots more photos from her parents' balcony and they would be much better than the ones on her phone. Still, this had never happened before.

There was a squirrel.

And the ginkgo trees.

But no turtles.

"Neil, I thought daddy was going to take you to the Chicago Zoo today after school let us out early?"

"Why didn't he?"Liffey asked, visibly alarmed at the discovery that there were no turtles in her photos and changing the subject.

"I don't know. We were on our way but he got a message beep in New Glarus right after we passed by that second plastic cow on the right. So he pulled off the road and looked at the message."

"Then he sent a text. Then he downshifted like a race car driver and just spun around. He made a U-turn and started *speeding* all the way home!"

81

"It was amazing! I had no idea daddy even *knew how* to do a U-turn! He dropped me off here because mom wasn't going to be home until late this afternoon. Which is great! I'm glad! This pond protection project is *way* better than any zoo."

"Next, after I find a place to put this owl, I get to unpack that big **'FRAGILE SKUNK'** box," he added enthusiastically.

"What skunk, Neil?" Aunt Jean asked, obviously perplexed.

"I have not ordered a skunk decoy, Neil. But now that you mention it, perhaps I should. Do they eat fish?"

Liffey's head began to pound and the deck started spinning as she lurched around, trying to grab on to something.

She staggered forward, struggling to reach a sturdy deck chair, overshot it and fell head first into the pond, slamming her head against a large rock on her way down.

Neil jumped immediately into the four foot pond. He quickly determined that Liffey's right arm had become wedged between two rocks on the bottom.

He did not have the upper arm strength to push one of the rocks out of the way so he could pull his sister's arm out from between them.

He knew he had to get Liffey out before she had brain damage—or worse.

Aunt Jean screamed and dialed 911 but before she could jump in to help her nephew, deputy trainee Patterson ran into the yard and jumped into the water with Neil who was jumping up from the bottom of the pond to take a breath and then immediately diving down again, trying to move the rock. The water was up past his shoulders.

Together, they quickly pushed one of the boulders to the side and gently lifted Liffey's arm. Deputy Patterson carried her out of the water.

He lowered her down on to the deck and was very relieved to note that she was conscious and breathing normally. It seemed she had inhaled very little, if any water.

Approaching sirens signaled that the local rescue squad and chief were on their way.

"We will have to send your niece to ER to have a look at that head injury," Officer Patterson said to Aunt Jean. "She's got quite a goose egg on the top of her forehead."

Aunt Jean placed a pillow under Liffey's head and wrapped her in the thermal blanket she kept on the deck for cold nights.

Liffey smiled and whispered "thanks," impressed that her aunt seemed to know what to do.

"How did you get here before I had disconnected my 911 call, officer?" Aunt Jean asked.

"He got here so quickly because he was following me," Liffey croaked.

Forgetting his deputy persona, Officer Patterson, visibly embarrassed, said: "How could you tell that I was following you Ms. Rivers?"

"Oh you did a very good job," Liffey reassured her rescuer. "I would never have noticed except I am used to trouble trailing me and I try to keep a step ahead of it when I can."

"There was one squirrel and there were supposed to be four turtles but only the squirrel was in the photos. There were no turtles. I just do not understand where the turtles went."

Officer Patterson tried to suppress the concern he felt regarding Liffey's head injury, after her incoherent comments.

Aunt Jean laughed uncertainly. Mercifully, before she could ask Liffey to explain what trouble she was talking about, the Chief of Police rushed into the yard, followed by Robert Rivers and two EMTs.

After a brief conference with Aunt Jean, the Chief gestured to his deputy to join him by the gate. "You are to follow the ambulance and remain at the hospital with Ms. Rivers until she is medically discharged into the custody of the FBI. You will stand outside of her room and protect her door."

"She will bypass ER and be immediately admitted to a regular hospital room. Her father will ride with her in the ambulance and remain inside her private room with her."

"When she is taken from her room for the head scan, you will continue your post at the door and her father will accompany her, along with two Sheriff's deputies."

"You are to admit no one into her room other than her parents, brother and aunt. Hospital personnel will have special passes. No exceptions. If someone does not have a pass, they are not permitted to enter the room—even while she is out getting her scan."

"If there is any resistance, arrest and handcuff that person immediately. Wear your gun. You have been trained for this kind of unlikely event at the police academy."

"Yes, sir," he answered, obviously confused and nervous.

"Am I to be apprised as to what is going on here?" he asked awkwardly.

"I can only tell you that she is in grave danger and Interpol has asked us to become actively involved with her safekeeping. She has an enemy that Interpol calls one of their phantoms because he is so difficult to out. He usually works alone."

"If he gains access to Ms. Rivers, without a doubt, he will kill her. He will also kill you if you are not vigilant. I will be outside the room, wearing a hospital maintenance uniform and mopping the hallway."

"One more thing. Put your bullet proof vest on right now—before Liffey is taken to the ambulance."

Officer Patterson tried not to look as confused as he felt. How could this young girl be on anyone's *hit* list? And how could his first day on the job just become even more stressful?

"We will be working with Interpol when they get here, which should be early this evening. The FBI is sending three agents from Milwaukee. I have called the Sheriff and asked for backup at the hospital."

"The Sheriff's deputies are already on their way and will meet you at the ambulance bay. They will walk you to her private room and remain there until they leave with Liffey for her scan."

"Then it's up to you—and me, in the hallway, to keep the room area secure. Other Sheriff's deputies will be positioned at exit doors. They will also patrol the ER waiting lobby."

"The order is, Officer Patterson, not to take this threat down—if possible."

"Interpol wants him alive. They have been tracking him for years but his conflict diamond smuggling operation is still apparently thriving."

Before Officer Patterson could ask the question, the Chief said: "This is not directly our problem. You have obviously heard of blood diamonds? Or conflict diamonds?"

He nodded slowly and answered: "I have. As I understand it, uncut diamonds from mines in Africa are smuggled out by workers and end up being sold on black markets. Money from the diamond sales is used to buy weapons to finance military takeovers in unstable governments."

The Chief nodded approvingly and continued his briefing.

"Well, this man is only coming for Liffey Rivers because he knows she can identify him. She stopped a blood diamond transaction in Saint Louis."

"She's got a kind of sixth sense and has been able to take evasive action. Her mother should be able to ID him too but when she knew him, she was very ill. She had amnesia and is missing years of her life. It's a sad story."

"Will I be leaving with Ms. Rivers when she is discharged?" Officer Patterson asked.

"I am not sure. I do not have any details as to how that will be coordinated yet."

"Anyway, after she has been discharged, her house will be under constant surveillance. She will not attend school and her only cleared outing in the foreseeable future is a limousine ride transporting her to and then back from O'Hare where she will pick up friends arriving from Ireland and New Jersey. Her father is dispatching his law office's limo for the trip."

"When the limo brings them back to Mineral Point, they will require a police escort if they go so far as out the back door of the Rivers' house. In case you are wondering, I do mean that literally. They are not to leave the house under any circumstances unless they have Interpol's clearance—and protection."

"When Interpol gets here, they will take over and the FBI agents from Milwaukee will leave."

"I am calling our part-time officers in for fulltime duty, starting tomorrow, until this situation has been resolved. We will do as we are told. I imagine it will be primarily guarding the Rivers' grounds."

Whatever it is, how could anything require four police officers on duty in Mineral Point at the same time? Officer Patterson thought uneasily.

It can't be the vampire incident, can it? Is the Chief now juggling a possible hit man attack on a young girl along with all the bus stop hysteria from this morning?

He worried now that perhaps he should not have mentioned the Wendigo haiku to that cashier earlier today and very much hoped that he had not interfered with the Chief's investigation by his unprofessional behavior.

What in the world had he been thinking when he had recited that haiku poem?

He did not even know the woman's name.

The haiku was police business. It was bad enough that the students' own stories from this morning had spread so quickly. But as far as he knew, the students did not know about that haiku. Only he and the Chief did—and possibly Attorney Rivers.

He began to sweat. His stomach began churning like a car engine that refused to turn over. He feared that he was going to be sick.

Today had been overwhelming. His first day alone on active duty and he may have already screwed up big time talking to that cashier–showing off.

First, there had been the Wendigo, or whatever it was, at the bus stop chaos.

Then the order to follow Liffey Rivers, followed by the rescue in the fish pond.

Third, his new assignment to protect Liffey Rivers. *Protect Liffey Rivers from a diamond smuggler? She's only a high school sophomore!*

He normally did not carry his gun but he headed for his squad car to get the weapon from the locked glove compartment as the Chief had directed.

And working with Interpol? An elite international policing agency? This was crazy! How could his first day on duty in a small, almost crime free, midwestern town, be so off the charts?

When he had applied for the fulltime police force in Mineral Point, nobody had told him he would be involved in Secret Service kind of protection.

He very much hoped that the Chief would fill him in soon, because this was not the kind of 'public service' he had envisioned when he had signed on.

The Chief was a fair guy though. He suspected the Chief was out of the loop too about the details of what was going on.

He walked slowly to his squad car to put the bullet proof vest on and retrieve his weapon, trying hard to believe that this was really happening.

Had he hurt his head today, like Liffey?

Opening the glove compartment, he took out the hand gun and immediately vomited all over the outside door of the passenger side of his vehicle.

He recovered quickly and went to the trunk to retrieve his bullet proof vest.

Something he could not have imagined he would ever need to wear in Mineral Point.

Overhead helicopter noises drew him away from his frightened state of mind. *Helicopters don't fly over Mineral Point he thought*—except the flight for life ones.

They are definitely not medical rescue helicopters. And they are heading in the direction of the hospital in Dodgeville.

He drew in a deep breath and exhaled. Working with the Feds on his first day on duty here in the middle of nowhere was a nightmare.

Those helicopters are almost *at the hospital,* he thought with great relief.

I will not be protecting this young lady alone. If only I had some idea of what I was protecting her from.

If this day got any more interesting, he was going to have a serious nervous breakdown.

INTERCONNECTIVITY

It seemed to Sister Mary Agnes, that the ocean of calm black storm clouds she often saw in the western sky as she walked the grounds, praying her rosary, were only waiting for a powerful wind to move them in her direction. Then, whatever it was that had been stalking her, would be unleashed.

Years ago, when her physical body started to wind down, her spiritual body began to experience altered states of consciousness while she was praying in the reliquary chapel, where she spent most of her time.

In the small chapel, among so many relics of the saints, her sense of time and space was often replaced by a state of euphoria. She was so consumed by God's love and the beauty of creation during these ecstasies, she sometimes felt like she was circling the sun in a chariot of fire.

Many years ago, a presentation had been given at Medikea Mound's continuing education lecture series, about the interconnectedness among all living things.

The presenter was a renowned French scientist who described how clumps of fungal threads are attached to tree roots like telephone wires.

Dr. Berenger said that these fungal threads enabled trees, even from miles away, to "talk" to each other, using an electrochemical communication system very similar to the synapses between neurons in humans.

He had presented a time lag documentary video that clearly showed how buffalo thorn trees in Africa, while giraffes were eating their leaves, had warned other trees through their fungi networks that there was danger. The trees that were warned, then closed their own leaves to make them less attractive to the giraffes.

Using the same kind of time lapse photography, other trees, that were being attacked by leaf-eating bugs, were also shown releasing chemical signals into their fungi network that enabled neighboring trees to pick up their signals and increase their own chemical resistance to the bug threat.

Apparently, Sister had come to understand, all trees had similar electrochemical communication systems. She was delighted to hear that there was a *bona fide* scientific explanation because she thought she might actually be tuned in to the mysterious communication network trees shared with each other.

She believed that was how she had discovered the young girl who was in so much mortal and spiritual danger.

For many years, while sitting on the patio bench between the two gingkoes, Mary Agnes had been able to feel the almost imperceptible electrical signals that the trees were emitting. For a long time, she thought that she was imagining it. Now she was certain that it was real.

Recently, there had been an upsurge of activity between the two gingkoes on the patio. Since she did not speak "Ginkgo" she had been, until recently, unable to discern what was going on.

One day, with no advance warning, while sitting on the old patio bench, she had suddenly found herself suspended above and between two other large ginkgo trees in an unfamiliar place.

She had no idea where she was or how she had gotten there. Her attention, after getting over the shock of being a disembodied spirit suspended above the ground, was drawn to a young girl beneath her, sitting cross-legged on a yoga mat, either deep in meditation, or sound asleep. It was hard to tell.

Dangling from the branches of both trees, there was a cluster of furry black spiders, descending on long black threads, like Halloween party decorations.

Thankfully, the girl was completely oblivious and had not detected them—even though there were two spiders suspended just a few inches away from her nose.

Sister Mary Agnes blessed herself. She recognized the repulsive spiders as preternatural manifestations. She had seen these spider creatures many times— usually crawling on the walls of her small bedroom. Sometimes on the ceiling. They were outward symbols of an infestation of evil. Spiritual bad energy in ghost form.

She knew that these spiders were not there to directly harm the girl. They were there waiting to feed on whatever it was that was coming for the girl, like flies drawn to manure in a field of cattle.

Mrs. Pembroke had wisely written down the haiku that the nice young officer had so graciously shared with her. She was glad she had done this, because now, she seemed to be the only true authority on that subject who was reachable.

The Chief of Police had disappeared, as had the nice young officer who had been kind enough to give her all of the facts.

Nancy Pembroke had become the apparent go-to authority on what was placed in the haiku box at The Foundry Books that morning.

Nancy had managed to quickly organize today's highlights in her head: there was a box turtle involved and very possibly a Wendigo attack coming soon. According to the students' reports, there was also a skeletal old man floating along the sidewalk in front of The Foundry Books and a handsome young man with long, dark hair.

It was hard to keep the facts straight. The whole town knew about the floating man and the running man with coal black hair and the puff of smoke and the vampire cape and the blast of frigid, vampire air. The students who had experienced those phenomena had blabbed that information all over the place, even though they had apparently promised not to discuss today's bizarre event. Most teens were predictably irresponsible.

But, as far as she knew, she had been the first civilian to learn about the Wendigo poem and the turtle.

The worst scenario here might be the end of the world.

She was looking forward to her hair appointment and manicure at the salon today before her press interviews. Unfortunately, there would not be time to squeeze in a pedicure.

Some of the students who had seen the vampire that morning, were also granting interviews. But she was the only one she knew of, other than the police, who knew about the threatening haiku. This was BIG and she was very excited to have played such an important part in the exciting, unfolding drama. The locals deserved to know the facts.

It was also good for local businesses with all the influx of people coming to look for the vampire. She was amazed that traffic in front of the Pointing Dog grocery had gone from the usual car every now and then, to a real traffic jam.

Frustrated drivers and their bored passengers had come into the supermarket, abandoning their hardly moving cars and purchased record numbers of snacks and take-out sandwiches. Even the greatly reduced day-old ones.

Most of the motorists made the same comment: "Why does everyone in Wisconsin seem to be in Mineral Point today?"

"Well, I suppose it's because of what happened here this morning at the school bus stop," Nancy told her eager listeners.

"I had a long chat with the policeman who was sent by the Chief of Police to buy fruit and hot dogs for the box turtle that the terrifying vampire had left on The Foundry Books porch, along with a threatening haiku poem predicting a time of sorrow and the coming of a Wendigo cannibal monster who will blot out the sun."

Because she had been foresighted enough to write down the haiku verses on a discarded grocery receipt, she was able to read the haiku poem verbatim for her audiences.

Sometimes as many as twenty-five people at a time listened to her story. She was, after all, almost an eye witness to the bizarre event which had occurred just a few hours ago in downtown Mineral Point.

And it has only just begun! she thought excitedly.

Nancy Pembroke marveled at the twists and turns of fate. Only that morning, she had been a grocery store cashier. Now she was the 'go-to' authority here in Mineral Point for exclusive, almost up-to-date information, about the mysterious paranormal event which had taken place at the school bus stop.

"I know even more than the students who actually saw the apparition," she told her mesmerized listeners.

Because of the haiku, she knew that there was a Wendigo attack coming soon. Or perhaps something even worse?

"Darkness erases the sun? Could this mean that the apocalypse is coming? The end of the world?" Nancy suggested to her audiences.

It had become her civic responsibility to spread the alert. Not that it would matter much if it really was going to be the end of the world.

She had no idea what "trees are whispering" meant. She had never liked poetry in school. It was very boring and never made much, if any sense. It was just plain dull. Especially the haiku poems. Although, if she were to be honest with herself, she could not recall having ever read a haiku poem before today and it had been anything but boring.

She hoped once again that she had not caused the present panic in Mineral Point. But what was done was done. She was looking forward to her on location television interview in front of The Foundry Books this afternoon where she would have an opportunity to set the record straight.

Some of the students who had seen the vampire that morning were also taping their statements. But she was the only one she knew of, other than the police, who knew about the threatening haiku. This was BIG and she was very excited to have played such an important part in the unfolding drama. The locals certainly were entitled to know their fate.

Mrs. Pembroke sincerely hoped that the nice young officer who had bought the hotdogs and berries that morning for the box turtle was not going to get in trouble when she revealed how she knew so much about the impending disaster in Mineral Point.

She knew she had promised him that she would not discuss the matter, but how could she not? She feared that Mineral Point, for some reason unknown to her, had been singled out for retribution by the vampire-Wendigo creature.

She might bring that possibility up during her interviews later today.

The police were always trying to keep people from panicking. So should Paul Revere and Sybil Ludington not have ridden their horses during the Revolutionary War to spread the alarm that the British were coming? She was warning *her* people that, "The Wendigo is coming!"

Nancy Pembroke considered for a moment, the possibility that she might be mentioned in history books someday.

Maybe there would be time at the salon for some blonde highlights too.

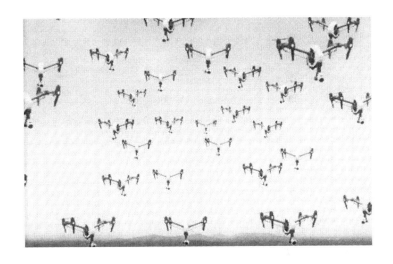

THE HOSPITAL

The Chief finally finished filling out his Liffey Rivers Incident Report, grateful that there were no more questions to ask Jean Rivers, who had very quickly exhausted his patience.

Her yard was the stuff of nightmares and he had insisted that she order a fence to be put up around the entire pond as soon as he left. The high gate was sufficient but another, equally high fence, also had to be erected immediately.

She seemed to think that the woods behind the fish pond provided "natural" as she had put it, protection from people's gaining access to the pond area. She was apparently more worried about fish predators, like blue herons, swooping down into the water and eating one of her koi fish, than children falling in the pond.

Posting **KEEP OUT** and **BEWARE** signs were not for the woodland animals, she had explained. They were intended to warn hikers on the public trails in back of her house to keep away.

The Chief decided her explanation was sound and could only hope that she did not actually believe her signs were deterring animals as well.

It was hard to tell how nuts this lady actually was.

Sane or otherwise, he did not have time to be patient with Jean Rivers. He had to get to the hospital.

He told her he would be back to personally inspect the fence no later than next Monday. He attached **DO NOT ENTER** police tape across the gate, thinking that he had not used this much tape in one day in his entire career in Mineral Point.

He ordered Jean Rivers to keep the tape there until she replaced it with a high fence within the next five days.

When she anxiously asked how her fish were to eat if she could not enter the pond area to feed them, he patiently replied: "You can enter Jean. This is your own property. This is not a crime scene."

En route to the hospital in Dodgeville, he called Ellie, the dispatcher, and reminded her to feed the turtle. Ellie told him that his hospital maintenance uniform was in locker A5 in the hospital employee's break room.

He increased his speed and turned his flashing police lights on. He had to get to the hospital before the ambulance to be dressed and in place when they brought the Rivers girl to her private room.

As he switched his siren on, he phoned his wife and told her that several emergencies had come up and that he knew nothing further about the Wendigo matter.

An odd sense of urgency had come over the usually laid back Chief Peter Smith. Like there was some kind of cataclysmic event unfolding and he was powerless to stop it.

He reached the hospital and parked in front of the emergency room. After he had asked the nervous-looking ER receptionist where the locker was located, he began his first undercover police assignment.

He hoped his new deputy was up for what might lay ahead. As if he had any idea what to expect himself. He felt like he had been cast as an extra in a movie as he exited the elevator with his cleaning cart, wearing a green hospital uniform, embroidered: Sam Martin.

The Chief could not help wondering if Sam Martin was dead and if this uniform might be an omen of what lay ahead for himself.

Banishing his morbid thoughts and relieved to see that Officer Patterson was already in place outside of Liffey Rivers' private room, he removed the cart's mop and got to work.

The hallway was empty. He could hear Robert Rivers talking in his daughter's room and hoped her aunt would not arrive anytime soon.

He hated to admit to himself that he was dreading this stakeout. He had never been on a real one before.

101

Even in uniform. Every hair on his arms bristled in anticipation of what might be waiting for him.

The suspense was suffocating.

As he made his way slowly down the hallway, he hoped he looked like he knew what he was doing.

The bucket of soapy water slurping around on this cart was intimidating, as was the floppy rag mop. He had obviously overfilled the bucket.

He wasn't sure how to swipe at the floor with the rag mop. Now, he feared that if he died today, he might be remembered as a chauvinistic pig who had never helped his wife around the house.

Looking around, he thought that if the FBI agents were in place, he saw no sign of them.

But that was probably good? Right? he asked himself.

Was it just going to be himself and the rookie, Patterson?

He wished now that he could go back in time when his biggest problem had been chasing down chickens in a school parking lot.

So much for Federal agents, the man in the blue uniform shirt labeled 'Hospital Security' thought, pulling the two unconscious FBI agents into the service elevator and jamming the door shut with a small screw driver. *This should provide sufficient time to take care of the girl.*

Knowing what a commotion the discovery of the two unconscious FBI law enforcement agents would create, he quickly removed the drone control device from his satchel and pressed: 'Activate.'

Plugging in the coordinates, he saw that it would be six minutes until it would be 'event time.' A single drone sounded like a bee. Fifty drones would sound like an invasion of buzz saws in a transformer movie.

He had planned to use these spider-like drones at a later time and date but they were replaceable within 24 hours and he needed the first batch today.

He positioned himself near a watercooler by an exit door and waited. When the drones arrived, they would create chaos for fifteen full minutes as they circled the hospital like vultures hunting for road kill.

Then they would land in nearby fields for a grand finale.

These diversions should give him sufficient time to administer the drug, take the girl from her hospital bed and transfer her to the wheelchair he had parked next to the visitors' elevator.

He would not take her life today.

After all the time and energy he had expended so far to eradicate the little pest, he wanted to move her in to his new tunnels for an extended visit to let her experience the frustration he had endured ever since St. Louis—because of her.

It was personal now.

She had lucked out at every twist and turn but not today. Interpol was not here yet or he would have heard their copters flying overhead and then noisily landing on the roof, so he had time.

There were only the two drugged FBI agents in the elevator and one local cop to deal with now—even though he strongly suspected the Chief of Police was probably wandering around the halls disguised as a hospital employee.

The Sheriff's deputies were in the parking lots and by the exit doors which could create a problem but the drone excitement should keep them occupied looking up until he could escape. His van was parked at the ER entrance in a Handicapped parking place.

He was glad he had thought to steal some orderly's scrubs from a locker. He needed to wear them to get the girl out of the private room and on to the gurney he had 'borrowed' from one of the ER cubicles before the real orderlies arrived to transport her to the scan.

There were only two minutes left to accomplish this before bedlam would ensue.

He had hacked into the hospital's daily procedures schedule and had determined the exact time for the diversion to begin.

Just when he was beginning to doubt his accuracy, he heard the drones. He had programmed them to fly in little V formations—like migrating geese.

He slowly walked down the hall towards the girl's room where the young officer, who was guarding the door, looked confused and frightened—just as he had hoped.

When he had almost reached the room, he was dismayed and furious that, instead of moving towards the hallway window to look out and observe the noisy drones, he saw the local police officer running into the room and slamming the door shut.

He could clearly hear the room's furniture being used to barricade the girl and whoever else was inside the room with the policeman, talking softly.

He also thought he saw a nun dressed in a white habit, suspended at least three feet in the air, watching him make his way down the hallway.

It had to be some kind of optical illusion but it still gave him the heebiejeebies.

The wig girl was slowly driving him crazy.

This nun had to be the result of some kind of long overdue psychotic 'break.'

This was something he had not expected though— a rookie cop, who apparently had good instincts. He had somehow recognized the drones as a diversion to divert his attention from guard duty.

So much for the hospital abduction.

He had badly miscalculated.

By depending almost entirely upon the nervous young officer he had seen throwing up on his police vehicle only a few hours ago, to run to the corridor window, he would now be forced to take the wig girl to her new home in the tunnels beneath Mineral Point—the *next time* opportunity came knocking.

It was always the *next time* with Liffey Rivers.

But those *'next times'* were running out.

She was now officially living on borrowed time.

The disturbing thing was, he had recently begun to feel like he too, was living on borrowed time, and that it was only a matter of very little time now until he might be seeing that nun again.

His mother had often told him bedtime stories about angels coming to get you when it is your "time."

SISTER MARY AGNES

When the stream of melting colors started to fade on the far side of the main chapel that evening, Mary Agnes began to tremble, signaling that her conscious mind was about to be hijacked—again.

Mary Agnes hesitated to discuss these trembling episodes, along with her communicating with trees theories, with her confessor. Any priest hearing her confession might dismiss her unsolicited visions as a symptom of some sort of serious mental illness. Or dementia.

She could obviously never mention the out of body experiences she was regularly having now either.

If she did, no one would believe her anyway. Thus, she had not confessed her sins to a priest for many years.

She was very old now and whenever she could manage to actually fall into a deep night's sleep, it usually did not last very long. But then, she had more or less lost track of time. It seemed that for as long as she could remember, time was irrelevant. Life had become one long continuum with seemingly no end in sight and no beginning recalled.

It was because the Latin word **VINDICTA** would begin scrolling through her brain like news scrolling along the bottom of a television screen, that Mary Agnes often found sleep so elusive.

It wasn't just the word **Vindicta,** the Latin word for revenge, that entered her mind, uninvited.

A life-like image of a box turtle hiding inside its shell always accompanied this frightening word. Sister Mary Agnes could never quite make out what the turtle was hiding from. However, she was positive that the terrible smell she detected during and after these recurring visions was the same stench present during the long ago exorcism in Japan. It was the smell of rotten meat.

When this vision would begin to recede, she often felt some of herself oozing out of her body, like a tiny blob of toothpaste being squeezed from its tube.

After sunset each night, Mary Agnes moved from the main chapel to the small, usually empty, reliquary chapel, directly across the hall, until the nurse assigned to her floor that night came looking for her, as she often did when Sister got lost in prayer. And if the

108

nurse did not come, so much the better because she would remain there in prayer all night.

She loved being in the small reliquary chapel filled with so many bits of saints' bones, each individually displayed and labeled under protective glass.

Sister did not turn the overhead light on in the chapel. She preferred the shadows cast by the candles in front of the statue of Saint Michael the Archangel, to the right of the main altar.

She was certain that her turtle vision, with its threatening message, needed her immediate and complete attention and it would take more than one night of prayer to sort it out. She began her prayers, invoking the Archangel Michael to "defend her in battle."

Vindicta? Who would be seeking revenge against such a young girl? Was she also in danger because she was praying for the girl? What good was having a psychic gift, if that is what she actually had, if she did not know how to interpret the images and subtle messages she regularly received like an old, discarded TV antenna?

Her knees snapped, crackled and popped like Rice Krispies as she struggled to get back up on to her feet again, taking care to place her walker directly in front of her.

Struggling not to dwell on the box turtle's revenge message and the snarling animal in the shadows in her recurring vision, she slowly started moving towards the front of the relic repository.

The turtle reminded her of the effigy mound in back of the former girls college on Medikea Mound.

The sisters had great respect for Native American culture. No one here at the Motherhouse would have disturbed it. *But I cannot find it lately when I look for it now on my mound walks. I will ask Sister Honoraria if she remembers....*

Another disturbing image came to her just before she reached the relic altar. She now saw the pattern on the box turtle's shell clearly and was very startled to recognize it as a familiar Japanese symbol.

She had been sent to Japan in her early twenties to work with victims who suffered from chronic health problems after the atom bomb had been dropped on Hiroshima.

These unfortunate people had already been sick for over two long years with radiation poisoning when she had arrived at Saint Benedict's Hospital.

This experience had badly scarred her for life— seeing so much physical pain and lingering spiritual despair and darkness had been overwhelming.

One of the patients at the hospital, a young man, had spent hours every day writing a word that Sister Mary Agnes had been able to find immediately in the only dictionary her convent's library had on hand: a thick 'Japanese To Latin' dictionary.

The Japanese symbols were: **復讐**

The two Japanese symbols translated into Latin was: **VINDICTA,** which meant **REVENGE** in English. Most people who spoke English would know what that word meant.

It is actually a lovely pattern design for a box turtle's shell, Mary Agnes thought, writing in her prayer journal about the turtle vision.

However, it is highly unlikely that this threatening symbol is the result of a mistake made by Mother Nature.

Whoever altered the turtle's shell is seeking revenge. It is a dark proclamation of some kind.

I must pray night and day for enlightenment as to who it is that needs prayer so urgently. I fear it is a matter of life or death.

Perhaps for both of us...

Of late it had become obvious to her that she did not have enough stamina to continue her life of intercessory prayer on earth much longer.

Sister Mary Agnes was both physically and mentally drained. She also hated to admit to herself that for the first time in her life, she was frightened.

She had assisted at an exorcism in Japan of the same young man who had spent his days scribbling the revenge message.

The ritual had lasted four long days and nights.

The terrible smell that had invaded the back room where they were conducting the ancient religious rite had almost caused the priests to stop their effort.

In the end, the man had fallen into a deep, peaceful sleep and when he woke up, he smiled and politely asked for a cup of tea.

111

From that day on, he no longer wrote the word **Vindicta** on the hospital walls.

The noxious rotten meat smell finally receded and the two weary Catholic missionary Jesuit priests were sleeping soundly on uncomfortable folding chairs when Mary Agnes returned to her convent, mortally exhausted.

It was 1947.

THE PRODUCER

The vast underground network of abandoned lead mines and tunnels running underneath Mineral Point was formidable. However, using a map from 1842 along with advanced electrical resistivity, it had been possible to not only locate most of the mines but also to adapt and fortify some of those tunnels.

Several other tunnels had also been shored up and had been transformed into comfortable living quarters for the Producer and four retired soldiers from the U.S. Army Corps of Engineers.

The only uncomfortable aspect of the tunnels was that people had been shorter in the mid-1800's than they were now and all but one of the engineers had to bend over as he worked.

This caused considerable back pain for the workers which the Producer countered with addictive, narcotic pain relievers which he personally administered twice daily.

After their evening gourmet frozen food dinners, the engineers were given sleeping pills which kept them accounted for until breakfast when they began the narcotic pain relievers.

There was fresh air being pumped in and recycled and a vast supply of gourmet frozen food and video games stored in their temporary home under the ground. There were also four new laptop computers and DVDs and CDs stacked as high as the five foot ceilings. These could be used during lunch and dinner.

Hiring four retired Army Corps of Engineers had been a stroke of absolute genius. Each of them had been trained at the Tunnel Warfare Training Center in California's Mohave Desert.

All four engineers were well acquainted with both the tunnels in Afghanistan, that led to mountain hideouts for the Taliban, as well as the much more luxurious tunnel networks in Iraq, which led to condo-like bunkers and supplies.

The maze of passageways in underground Mineral Point, some connected, others not connected, had been abandoned for many years, and had presented a unique challenge for the Producer. There was lead contamination to deal with and most of the tunnels needed major work.

There were two networks of tunnels that were being restored. One tunnel, which connected to the

Rivers' property, and a more extensive network near The Foundry Books. Some of those were used to store the Producer's props. Others were the living quarters of the engineers.

The Producer had paid an unbelievable amount of money to his engineers to build the underground 'realistic set' of what they were told would be a major Hollywood movie to be released sometime late next year.

In exchange for signing a total secrecy clause and other strict contractual rules and regulations regarding their involvement with this unique project, each of them would be paid $500,000 after work on the tunnels was completed.

The remarkable thing, was that all that money was to be earned without having to risk their lives as they had done while in the Army working underground in hostile enemy territory.

Another remarkable thing, was that none of the four engineers would ever see that money because the unwritten, but still binding clause, left out of their contract with the Producer, was that upon completion of the tunnel project, their brain chemistry would be permanently altered by a few special pills and they would have no memory of the Mineral Point tunnel work. It would be as if it had never happened.

The engineers were ecstatic. This time, there would be no one waiting to kill them in the tunnels. All they had to do was what they had been trained to do: fortify the four connecting tunnels which would be used as the realistic set for the still untitled movie and build luxurious living quarters for themselves and their employer while they worked.

The Producer's office and sleeping quarters were to be part of the tunnel system too. He insisted that he needed to be on site at all times and had temporarily closed his Hollywood office.

For the experienced engineers, it was like child's play, even though they were well aware that hidden mine shafts, rotten timbers, poisonous gases and unstable explosives could be waiting for them down in subterranean Mineral Point.

Because of an existing 1842 Mineral Point map and current technology, it was safe to say that it was not a 'mission impossible' scenario that the Producer was organizing.

His four engineers had three months to complete the project and would receive big bonuses if they finished it ahead of time. The Producer had amassed all the supplies they would need to reinforce three chambers of a large underground mine directly across the street from The Foundry Books. He stored the supplies in a building above the mine which he had anonymously purchased.

This movie would be a blockbuster and would certainly be a contender for an Academy Award. The Producer told his engineers he had hired "major talent" to star in this film. It was to be a vampire movie and he told the engineers that they were going to be an integral part of the film.

They were not permitted to contact anyone in the outside world and therefore had no internet or cell phone access down in the tunnels where they were working. Since it was only a three month project, the engineers were not concerned about being literally locked in 24 hours a day while they worked. Each of them had experienced far worse during their tenure overseas.

They had been carefully screened by the Producer who had also hired several private detectives to do extensive background checks.

Unlike most background checks, designed to flush out the sanest, fittest and most qualified candidates, he wanted only loners and misfits with borderline to mild personality disorders to be considered for this project.

The Producer provided his workers with special lighting that was used in sunless Scandinavian winters to help prevent or treat seasonal affective depression. Depressed laborers would slow down his project.

He also insisted on vitamin D supplements and provided nutritious meals and snacks throughout the day. Food supplies were delivered under cover of darkness at the abandoned building.

After studying the old 1842 map, the Producer found it hard to believe that anyone actually still risked living in Mineral Point. He had used an Electrical Resistivity report done by a graduate student in engineering at the University of Wisconsin that mapped Mineral Point's network of abandoned lead mines. Since it had been the student's doctoral dissertation, the Producer was confident it had been done thoroughly and competently.

There was so much limestone and sandstone in so many places, it was very possible that the tunnels would eventually collapse and turn into deadly sink holes as the ground in the area had been unstable for centuries.

However, the Producer's four project engineers were not worried about limestone and sandstone. Compared to what they had all been through in Iraq and Afghanistan, this assignment seemed like playing house.

It was also very exciting being such an integral part of a major motion picture. They were already planning the limo they would rent for its Hollywood debut. Maybe one painted in classic camouflage. There was talk of hiring an agent when the time came. Maybe they could also get a speaking part in the movie? As soon as they saw a script, they would have to discuss this further with the Producer.

The Producer's next sensational 'event' would make the Wendigo sighting pale in comparison. The locals would prefer a flesh-eating monster scenario to what he had planned for "Part Two."

He tried not to dwell on how many "final Liffey Rivers scenarios" he had carefully designed and tried to execute.

During his Liffey Rivers extermination campaigns, he had been having the worst luck imaginable. Uncannily bad, horrible luck. He tried not to keep fixating on the subject, but he could not fathom how he had not been able thus far to end this pathetic drama. All he wanted to do was rid the planet of the wig freak.

Maybe her mother too. It was true she might be able to identify him like her daughter could, but she had been an amnesiac during their association and his attorneys had assured him that they could easily have her identification testimony thrown out of court if it ever came to that.

It was her daughter that could positively identify him. She needed to be gone yesterday. To make certain that he would not have to face another futile attempt trying to eliminate her, he had given this Wendigo theme all of his attention. It was going to work this time—thanks to the tunnels under this charming Midwestern town—and his meticulous preparation.

After he had barely managed to escape from the authorities in St. Louis, it should have been all over. But the wig girl knew what he looked like. She had studied his face in the hotel lobby and forced him to flee the hotel like a common criminal.

When he had regrouped, she turned up at a feis in rural Ireland and caused complete havoc. Again he had somehow managed to get away in spite of the all points bulletins in place to capture him.

Then, after the Rivers girls managed to find each other again on top of a mountain in Ireland, he had been thrown off his horse, over a cliff.

He had survived, he liked to think, because he was resilient. The truth was, that he had lucked out because he had landed in a clump of soft needled pine trees.

When he had activated a distress signal from his wristwatch which pinpointed his exact location, he had been found two hours later by his Irish diamond connection associates.

The three rescuers had taken him to Sligo General Hospital where his broken arm was tended to. Before the hospital ER could complete their intake, he had vanished along with his rescuers.

Back in South Africa, after he had regained his bearings, he decided to 'job out' and he hired an expert herpetologist to rid his world of the wig girl by priming a black mamba snake.

But that did not work either. Instead, the plot had backfired and afterwards the would-be assassin had died on an airplane. 'LR,' as he called the pest, had actually taken out his half-million-dollar hit man by herself.

When he thought about this, it still gave him heart palpitations.

Finally, he once again tried to get rid of her himself. He had altered his physical appearance and erased his fingerprints. He then booked an economy cabin on a cruise ship where his sources had told him the Rivers family had the use of The Alaskan Sun's VIP quarters, belonging to the ship line's owner. Maeve Rivers had designed the elaborate suite.

Disguised and successfully eluding Interpol agents who were all over the boat, it had been a cheap thrill kind of cat and mouse game until there had been an unexpected polar bear attack and another major injury

120

setback when he was tossed into the Arctic Ocean by the giant bear.

After he had straddled the shoreline for several miles in his insulated wet suit, he floated back to the rocky beach and waited for pick-up.

Dealing with Liffey Rivers was like trying to eliminate a bad flea infestation. Twice he had hired experts who had promised results but they had been as unsuccessful as he had been to date.

This time, he was going to take as much time as he needed to finish off the wig girl and possibly her mother—although he did still have a soft spot for Maeve Rivers who had been terminally ill when he found her abandoned on a small jungle runway, half dead and completely out of her mind.

That she had believed everything he told her for years afterward was incredible.

Ironically, the nuns in the jungle hospital who had nursed her back to health and cured her of the cancer in her body, could not help their patient's amnesia.

He had told the nuns and fragile Maeve, that she was his sister, and that they, brother and sister, had taken over control of their deceased parents' diamond import business.

He had no idea who she really was. Nor did he care. He suddenly, out of nowhere, had a clueless assistant diamond executive. And although she had no long-term memory, she was very bright and had proved herself to be a quick learner.

For eight years, she had unknowingly smuggled thousands of blood diamonds over many borders—until her meeting with Liffey Rivers in Chicago.

That had changed everything. Now her mind had been restored and she had been reunited with her family.

The Producer was prepared to hunker down in Mineral Point, Wisconsin, for as long as it would take to regain his old life and some of the sanity he had lost while trying to deal with Liffey Rivers.

His diamond smuggling operation was now in a shambles due to the Rivers family's meddling and Robert Rivers cozy relationship with Interpol. He would deal with each of the Rivers separately, starting with Liffey.

There was more than enough room in the caverns and deep pits under Mineral Point for the entire Rivers family to spend their eternity.

Well-placed sources had recently alerted him that it was only a matter of time when he was going to be Interpol's top priority.

Therefore, he needed to be as invisible as possible. So he had moved underground in Mineral Point, Wisconsin, with his four army corps of engineers and his plans to take out the Rivers family.

He still had two weeks before the total eclipse of the sun would usher in his grand finale. After it was over, he would leave the wig girl and her unfortunate friends in what his engineers had told him was an "unstable and probably by now a sink hole mine." Down in that abyss, she would have plenty of time to reflect about what she had done to his life. And how little was left of her own.

The only thing that bothered him now, was that nun who kept randomly turning up in his nightmares with her translucent white face and staring eyes, like some kind of sniffer dog searching for his soul.

Recently, he had started dreaming about her almost every night—at least he thought he was dreaming. He would wake up and see her standing in the corner staring at him, her white habit sometimes shimmering with multiple faces, like it was difficult for her to appear as a one nun entity.

Always though, as soon as he stood up to confront her, she disappeared.

He had no idea why this nun was lurking around at night, but it made him feel uneasy.

Knowing that the 'problem' would soon be resolved once and for all, kept him going.

Maybe when the girl and her family and soon to arrive friends were gone, the nun would leave him alone.

If this nun was trying to make him feel guilty about his plans for Liffey Rivers and her entourage, it was not working.

He no longer believed in fairy tales and holy nuns.

It was all nonsense. He had chosen the dark side long ago and had no desire to reform. He had more money than most of the national treasuries in the small countries he normally did business with.

On the other hand, he liked to cover all his bases. Maybe the next time the nun turned up uninvited, he could get her to talk to him.

It would be worth a try.

She was making him very uncomfortable.

He could not remember the last time he had a good night's sleep.

There was always a new nightmare to deal with.

Between Abaddon and that nun, he felt like he was in a vise, being squeezed to death.

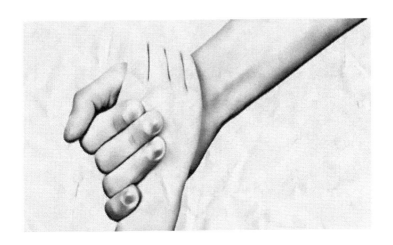

AN ALLY

Liffey was not happy about having to pick up her friends in a chauffeur-driven limo but there was no other choice. Neither of her parents could do it that day and John promised his mother that Aunt Jean would not be driving. That left a limo or taxi and Mineral Point did not have taxis. Her father had a limo.

The chauffeur would be for this trip only.

Liffey did not fault John's mother for worrying about Aunt Jean being the designated driver to and from O'Hare Airport.

His mother had met her aunt on The Alaskan Sun cruise. One night, Aunt Jean had told everyone at the dinner table, that the expression 'calving,' used for describing the process icebergs undergo losing big chunks of ice, did not mean that they actually gave birth to baby cows. Liffey could tell that John's mother was totally freaked out.

She could still recall Mildred Bergman's nervous laugh and the strained look on her face.

Liffey knew how seriously weird her aunt was, but sometimes her aunt actually did tell lame jokes. Liffey chose to believe that the icebergs calving, was one of them.

Whatever was or was not wrong with Aunt Jean, Liffey was fully resigned to the chauffeured limo arrangement, even though it made her feel like she was showing off.

The night before her guests arrived, Liffey could not sleep. She had remained on the edge of consciousness all night. Her dream cycles featured mini nightmares.

The floating nun had turned up again, this time with her hands folded in prayer and holding a box turtle. She would have to look for this new turtle in the big leaf lugularia plants.

There would be five turtles now if this dream turtle joined the other four. She had become very attached to the yard turtles and hoped they would stay in the vicinity of the ginkgo trees—even though she had discovered that the turtles were not real.

Since they had never turned up in the hundreds of pictures she had taken of them in the backyard, they were either figments of her imagination, or, as she suspected, from another dimension.

Liffey had explained to her mother, when Neil had informed Maeve that Liffey had taken turtle pictures that had no turtles, that obviously, "she had not been concentrating."

Her mother looked long and hard at her daughter, not believing Liffey's explanation. Liffey had taken hundreds of photos with the expensive camera over the years.

By 10:00 a.m. Liffey had given up entirely on sleep being a viable option for her. She had tried to sleep for the past twelve hours. However, she was not ready yet to dress for her trip to Chicago. She went outside and sat under the ginkgoes, hoping the turtles would visit—and they did. But there were only four.

So the turtle the nun had been holding had only been a dream turtle after all.

Liffey closed her eyes, enjoying the warm, gentle end of Indian Summer air. She was drifting off into a peaceful, meditative state, when she was startled by large clumps of ginkgo leaves falling on her from both of the ginkgo trees.

Liffey could clearly see that the oak and maple trees on the other side of the yard were not dropping their leaves. It was just the two ginkgoes.

Before she could figure out what was happening, the ginkgoes began shedding their leaves like Mother Nature was doing the Heimlich maneuver on them.

It was hard to stand up with an avalanche of leaves suddenly raining down on her. It almost seemed like the ginkgo trees were trying to bury her alive. She was frightened and decided she would try to stand up as

127

soon as the leaves reached her mouth. It felt like she was in the middle of a tornado.

Leaves blinded her until they had reached her shoulders, when they finally slowed down.

And then there were none.

She looked up and was astonished to see that the ginkgo trees were completely bare.

Not so much as one leaf dangled from a twig.

Liffey sat contemplating what had just happened. She had read about the unexplainable phenomenon of ginkgoes sometimes dropping all of their leaves at once. But, just like seeing the box turtles, she had never expected to see it actually happen. Of course, there was also the question of whether or not the box turtles in the yard *had* actually happened.

She leaned backwards into the sea of yellow leaves and noted that, although they had changed their color to yellow, the leaves were still fresh. It was not like they had been withering away and were ready to fall from the trees.

When she looked up at the bare branches for the second time, she saw the face of her ally, the nun in the white habit.

THE EYES OF THE ENEMY

Liffey was dismayed to discover that she was unable to settle down in this limo and get some of the sleep she had missed the night before. She doubted she had slept even two hours straight through. She felt like she always did when she studied for final exams. Vacant and queasy—edgy, like she was coming down with the flu.

Even though she had read about how ginkgo trees sometimes shed all their leaves at once—how likely would it be that both trees did this at the exact same moment? It was seriously strange. She made up her mind to find out more about the ginkgo tree event after her friends visit. Somehow it all seemed other worldly. But then she was seeing the floating nun often now. And mysterious turtles. She might be as crazy as her Aunt Jean now.

Liffey was very preoccupied and also very nervous. That was because she had been so looking forward to

John's visit, that now that the day had arrived, she was a bit apprehensive. Being totally sleep deprived did not help her state of mind. She had to admit though, that the two ginkgoes shedding their leaves like that had unnerved her. It had seemed apocalyptic.

Liffey was disappointed that Susan Scott had opted out of going with her to Chicago since she too knew John from last November's events in Mineral Point. However, it was not unexpected. Susan was doing her best to distance herself.

Susan had made up a lame excuse about having to help her dad rake leaves to the curb. Like that couldn't wait another day. Like Liffey was really supposed to believe that?

Liffey was very grateful that her friend Sinéad was making the reunion journey from Sligo. Since she was on The Alaskan Sun cruise ship with Liffey, she also knew the Bergman twins. Also, since Sinéad was an Irish dancer, she would be an honest critic as to how well prepared Liffey was for the Chicago Feis next weekend.

Liffey was grumpy and disoriented when she abruptly woke up after a short nap. Something was troubling her.

Things seemed to be "off" somehow.

Something was wrong.

It was the chauffeur.

It was also the limo.

To begin with, this chauffeur had not introduced himself. Liffey had seen him standing outside, leaning on the limo when he had arrived to pick her up—smoking a cigarette. Most limo drivers would be fired for smoking if word got back to their superiors.

Also, Liffey had opened her own limo door. She certainly had not minded—except that it was a limo gesture that every chauffeur she had ever encountered before had done routinely. It was part of the limo 'experience.'

Her father's four limos had only glass partitions separating front and back seats. He always laughed about how his fleet was not in the "party business."

Liffey could see that this limo had two partition options—glass and solid partitions. The chauffeur and backseat passengers both had buttons they could control for either option. The solid partition was down when Liffey had entered the limo. However, she had not noted it until now—even though this would have signaled that this limo was not part of her father's fleet.

So why, if there was so much police protection surrounding her now, did everything feel like *déjà vu?* There were the dreaded creepy crawly sensations that she always had when there was some kind of imminent threat or danger present—mixed with painful pins and needles running up and down her spine.

It was almost as if....

Liffey stopped breathing when her eyes met the lifeless lizard eyes staring at her in the driver's rear view mirror. The chauffeur had opened the glass partition while she had been sleeping. He had obviously been watching her in the mirror when she had finally drifted off.

There was not the slightest doubt in Liffey's mind that those eyes belonged to her worst nightmare.

Somehow she suppressed the urge to scream and desperately tried not to show any obvious signs of recognition. She had to make herself think clearly if she were going to have any chance of surviving this trip to O'Hare Airport.

She flashed a polite little smile which might give her a slight chance to bluff her way through this until she could figure out what to do.

Trying not to drown in the tidal wave of despair washing over her, she bit her bottom lip hard, and determined not to let on that she knew that the eyes which were staring at her now were probing, trying to determine whether or not she recognized them.

Was he plotting to take her somewhere other than O'Hare? Or was he planning to pick up her friends and then drive all four of them to some place she could not bear to think about at the moment?

She closed her eyes and pretended to go back to sleep while she frantically tried to come up with some kind of escape plan. If she did not keep her head on straight, she was not going to be alive to greet her friends at O'Hare Airport.

Making a big show of covering herself with the seat's blankets and arranging the pillows, she slowly positioned herself closer to the control buttons for the privacy options. This would be a logical thing for anyone to do if they wanted to continue sleeping. She pressed the solid partition button. It should not arouse his suspicion that she knew who was driving this vehicle. Anyone who wanted to sleep would want the solid partition down.

The solid partition button no longer worked. There was now no privacy. There was only the glass barrier separating passenger and chauffeur.

Liffey turned on her side away from the rear view mirror. Under her re-arranged blankets, she found out that her phone would not send. She kept getting error messages. She also discovered that she had no internet service. How had this happened?

Next, she felt her wrist and was elated she had not forgotten to wear her SOS bracelet that had GPS tracking and would let her parents know where she was at all times.

She pulled the little emergency plug on the bracelet but nothing happened. The GPS signal was gone. It was as dead as she was going to be soon if she did not figure out what to do. No phone. No SOS device. She was literally doomed.

Liffey was afraid she was going to faint. The Skunk Man was her chauffeur and he had jammed her phone and her only other GPS device. She was never going to see her good friends again. Or her parents or brother or Aunt Jean. Or Max or…

There were not many options available in a car going at least 65 mph on a three lane highway. They must be on Interstate 90 in Illinois by now. They had been traveling for well over two hours already and she was still totally blank and terrified.

Was this how it was all going to end? Her worst nightmare doesn't sneak into her house and kidnap

133

her—he just sits in a limo her *father* had lined up and she steps inside it and closes the door?

Like a zombie?

How could this be happening?

What had she been doing all this time?

Just sitting here in the backseat waiting for her execution to take place?

She had to fix this. If she did not, she would not live until sunset.

If she did risk jumping out of the limo, she would be immediately run over by another speeding car. Besides, this limo was most certainly not going to stop to pay tolls—it would fly past the toll booths in the I-Pass lanes. There would be no opportunity to scream, "Help!" at a manned toll station.

Since she most certainly did not have the physical strength to take over this limo, she needed to think of something else that might, unlikely as it might seem, actually work.

Liffey realized that she had very few, if any good options.

She was not sure she was up to today's survival test. This was easily the most life-threatening position she had ever been in.

HOW had this happened? She had gotten into this limo and was well on her way before she realized that her internal antenna had picked up danger. By then, it had been too late.

If only she had not been thinking about John and the others. Her head had been so clogged up with daydreaming, that she had been oblivious of any early warning signals she might have otherwise picked up on.

Maybe he would take a local exit and when he slowed down, she could risk opening the door and bolting before the limo accelerated again.

Then she remembered that limos lock the back doors from the driver's seat panel. This was to prevent drunken or suicidal passengers from doing exactly what she was hoping to do—jump out of the moving vehicle.

For some reason, Liffey was not nearly as surprised and terrified as she had always imagined she would be if this evil man ever managed to get hold of her.

She had always suspected, even though she had watched the attack happen in real time, that the Skunk Man had not really died when she saw a huge polar bear bat him into the Arctic Ocean.

Why else had her father built the safe house and continued to work with Interpol?

With so many officials searching for his body and never finding one, it was obvious others thought he was still alive too.

Her father pretended she was still a clueless little girl and she went along with it because she knew it helped to keep him sane.

Her mother knew that Liffey knew the worst, but also had not told this to Robert Rivers. They both tried to help him cope.

Still pretending to be asleep, her mind raced at warp speed trying to think of something she could do to save herself and her friends, when it came to that.

O'Hare would be the place she would need to stage a loud scene to get attention to her plight. However, she strongly suspected she was not going to make it to O'Hare. In a way, she hoped not. She did not want her friends to…

Why would the Skunk Man want the others?

He could dump her somewhere after he…and that would be the end of it.

Her family and friends would never really know what had happened to her.

Her parents, had she been able to reach them, would have contacted every policeman in Chicago by now and by the time she arrived at the airport, there would be an immediate rescue plan in place.

Liffey was already imagining how her devastated parents would be blaming themselves for letting this happen, when she realized that she was not alone in the backseat anymore.

THE MELTDOWN

She slowly moved her head, cracked her eyes open into tiny slits and saw a spot of white light on the seat next to her. Like someone had aimed a small laser beam there.

Then there were streaks of light and finally, the floating nun from the ginkgo trees was sitting next to her. She appeared to have many partial faces and had tripled her size, but it was definitely the ginkgo nun.

The instant this happened, the chauffeur looked into the rearview mirror again and cursed when he saw the nun who had been stalking him. How had that old ghost managed to get into this limo in broad daylight?

Until this moment, she had only been an illusion that had appeared in his nightmares. She was not real, but it looked like she was melting. She had numerous faces now but no body shape. She looked like she had exploded. He could not imagine what she was doing in this limo with the wig girl.

Unless.... He had considered the possibility over the past three years, that Liffey Rivers must have supernatural powers to have been so successful in thwarting all of the traps he had set for her. And now, here was this same ghost nun from his nightmares sitting next to her in the back seat, swelling up like a hot air balloon. It couldn't just be a coincidence.

At home in South Africa, Liffey Rivers would be called a Tokoloshe—an evil spirit.

He signaled a lane change and headed for the shoulder of the road, drastically decreasing speed as he maneuvered the limo onto the next exit ramp. He was going to dump the nun and get out of there.

As the limo slowed and entered the 'Emergency Stopping Only' shoulder of the road, the nun began to swell even more—like someone was pumping helium gas into her.

When the nun could barely fit in the backseat, the limo came to a full stop.

Liffey jumped out of the left hand door which was miraculously unlocked and tore away from the limo, waving her arms frantically at the on-coming traffic.

Cars slowed down but only one pulled off the road to help. A bald, middle-aged, uniformed policeman, got out of the unmarked car, flashed his badge and gestured for her to get into his police vehicle with its red and blue lights flashing in the rearview window.

Liffey was sure that she herself had now, as her father often said his sister Jean had done long ago, "gone over to the other side to live with the fairies."

While the Skunk Man's white limo was speeding away, the policeman who had rescued her was talking on his police radio while he tried unsuccessfully to shoot out the back tires on the escaping limousine.

Liffey was trembling and her teeth kept clicking together. The officer tried to reassure her and showed her his badge once again. He covered her shoulders with a small blanket and gently sat her down in the front passenger seat.

"Your father hired several off duty police officers to follow that limo to and from O'Hare. I picked up the tail at the Illinois border and until this incident, had planned to stay behind you to O'Hare and then back to the Illinois-Wisconsin border where an off-duty Wisconsin State trooper would take over and follow the limo back to Mineral Point. Looks like your dad suspected that something like this could happen. Do

139

you have any idea who that man was driving your limo?

"Have you seen him before?"

Liffey hesitated and then nodded her head, "yes."

"Do you know his name?"

"No," Liffey answered truthfully. "I'm sure he has many names."

"Well then, did you happen to see where that huge nun in the white habit went? She was standing in the middle of the road gesturing for the limo to stop when it ran right over her."

Liffey shook her head, "No Officer, I did not see it happen."

"Okay then. I am going to call your parents now and tell them what happened. We have an all-points bulletin already in place for that limo. He most likely won't be able to get through our dragnet, but if somehow he does and decides to get lost in traffic at O'Hare, Airport Security will find him. Roadblocks coming and going are being set up around the airport's perimeter."

"I have also been told the Feds are working this. They always do when a kidnaping is involved." *And when an Interpol most wanted criminal is involved*, Liffey thought, nodding politely.

"Officer, he was bringing me to the airport to pick up friends. They need to know they have to get protection and find a safe place right away because he is supposed to pick them up right outside of the International Terminal where my friend Sinéad McGowan, is arriving from Dublin. My other friends,

140

the Bergman brothers, are arriving from New Jersey. I have tried to reach all of them but he has done something to my phone and I cannot send or receive calls."

"Do you have a picture of each of them?"

Liffey quickly retrieved her phone and found a photo of her three friends in her photo gallery.

"My mother can send this from our PC at home, Officer. She has it on her Facebook page and my phone is still jammed."

"Why would he want to abduct your friends?" the policeman asked, putting his gun back in its holder.

"Because he knows if he has them, I will surface again, looking for them," Liffey answered matter-of-factly.

The policeman smiled. *Of course. She will deal with what Interpol described as an extremely dangerous madman and rescue all her friends. Sure. I will humor her and contact her mom after I file this incident report. The perp wanted her—not her three friends.*

The Producer knew he had only a few minutes before every cop on duty north of the Loop would be looking for his limo. And he was still three miles from O'Hare.

He needed to do damage control immediately.

Thankfully, he had exited the highway before it had become riddled with roadblocks.

When he turned onto County Road R, he was relieved to see in his rear view mirror, that there was no one in pursuit yet.

141

Search helicopters were no doubt already taking off from nearby heliports. They would be able to easily spot the white limo if he did not act quickly.

He was determined to put the nocturnal nun, who had just morphed into the melting blimp nun, and then disappeared entirely in broad daylight, while he drove right through her, entirely out of his mind.

Because, when he thought about what he had just witnessed, he doubted his sanity.

He left County Road R when he saw a single lane, dirt road, which ran alongside a harvested corn field. The road was probably used for farm equipment.

At the first thicket of trees, he pulled off the dirt road, hoping that the trees and bushes were sufficient to shield his long vehicle from view of passersby on County Road R.

However, the greater danger would come from the sky. He knew he could not risk staying here more than a few minutes and began emergency measures.

He switched on the limo's extensive system of heating coils and fixed the temperature at 96 degrees. Thanks to thermochromic, heat reactive paint, he still had a chance to get out of this mess.

It would only be a matter of minutes now until his white limo vanished and the olive green colored one appeared. He used a remote control license plate flipper to flip the front and back license plates while the body of the limo heated up and began to change color.

While the limo was turning camouflage green, he took a lighter and burned his driver's license and old limo permits. Then he scattered their ashes.

He placed the new documents, reflecting the new front and back license plates, into his wallet.

He was confident he could elude detection—if he moved quickly. No one would suspect a green limo of being the same white limo in which Liffey Rivers had almost been successfully abducted only minutes ago. He hardly believed the paint technology himself.

He checked the flight arrivals at the airport and noted that Liffey's guests had landed but they were not yet at their gates.

He undid John Bergman's phone jam and placed a call as he back tracked to County Road R in his new green vehicle.

When John answered, he was told by the chauffeur to: "Wait in front of your terminal door and we will be able to get out of O'Hare quickly. Apparently there is some sort of terrorist threat going on and traffic is going to be bad soon."

When John told him that Sinéad had already joined him and his brother, the chauffeur rejoiced. There was not one extra second to spare.

Before John could ask the chauffeur if he could speak with Liffey, the chauffeur cut in, "Good. I will be arriving in approximately eight minutes. Watch for me. I have a sign."

He did not really have a sign but it sounded like something a good chauffeur might say. He needed to remember to tell one of his Chicago connections to

143

untie Robert Rivers' chauffeur who had been drugged and was now tied up in the Rivers limo intended for today's O'Hare pickups. It was in a repair garage on Halstead. He had covered the sleeping driver with a warm blanket even though the weather was balmy and warm.

The chauffeur realized he was flying by the seat of his pants now and that he would need the wig girl's luck to get him through this. But he had a hunch it was going to work and he always followed his hunches.

He contacted his tech support and made sure that the Bergman brothers' phones were dead along with Sinéad McGowan's and of course, Liffey Rivers' two mobiles. He knew she always carried an extra one in case of emergencies.

The true disaster, would be if word got from Liffey to her parents about her fear that he would go to the airport without her and shanghai her friends, which was, of course, exactly what he was going to do.

He floored the accelerator, while keeping a sharp lookout in the sky ahead and behind him, for police helicopters.

Smiling broadly, the chauffeur opened the back door of the limo and invited John and Luke Bergman, along with Sinéad McGowan, to make themselves at home.

After apologizing for not disclosing on the phone earlier that Liffey was home in bed with a migraine headache and wanted to rid herself of it before their rendezvous, he added, pulling away from the curb:

"All of the beverages are complimentary and there are hors d'oeuvres in the small refrigerator. Please feel free to help yourself. You might particularly enjoy the non-alcoholic champagne. As you can see, it's on ice in the bucket and there are three glasses set out for you. Liffey tearfully asked me to make sure that I had this ready for you when I arrived at O'Hare. She is devastated she could not clear up her headache in time to come along. She asked that you include her in your celebratory toast."

He snapped a crisp, military salute to the passengers in his rear view mirror and locked all the limo doors automatically. Smiling ear to ear, he merged the olive green limousine into the outermost lane of O'Hare Airport Exits.

To Be Continued...

The Mystery of the Whispering Trees
Part II

www.liffeyrivers.com

ABOUT THE AUTHOR

Brenna Briggs is the author of eight Liffey Rivers Irish Dancer Mysteries and Mothers Addicted to Irish Dancing: MAIDS. Her books are included in the Irish Traditional Music and Dance Archive, Taisce Cheol Dúchais Éireann in Dublin. She has published humorous essays and short stories for Irish American magazines and newspapers and has been a guest speaker at many Irish Festivals and gatherings throughout the United States and Ireland. Born in Pittsburgh, Pennsylvania, she now lives in the Driftless Area of southwestern Wisconsin. Prior to this, she spent five years in County Sligo, Ireland, where she began writing The Liffey Rivers Irish Dancer Mysteries.

www.liffeyrivers.com

Made in the USA
Lexington, KY
13 April 2019